CW01677903

The Empath

By K. M. Simmons

In loving memory of Eula Mae Hutchins, Renee Hutchins, and Ollie. You were all loved and you're all greatly missed. Rest in paradise.

My mind was open before my eyes were. That is, I knew exactly where I was and who was nearby. My back sank into an old cotton mattress and my neck, arched upwards, lay still against lumpy feather pillows. A familiar presence was near and her scent filled my nostrils. I breathed it in, then let it go: Lavender; The flowers. The color. The scent.

Mama.

I was in my room, laying down in my mildly uncomfortable bed and my mom was near me.

"Uugh..."

A weak moan moved through my throat and escaped my lips. Gently I opened my mouth, little by little, and then quickly shut it. My mouth and my throat were as dry as the Sahara Desert.

Next, I tried to move my head. Left, right, then down. It barely moved. My aching neck was stiff and asleep. How long was I out?

And my head, God, my head. It felt like fireworks were going off. The melodic beat of drums banged against my temples. It felt as if my brain was trying to push through my skull.

Why don't you just open your eyes? I asked myself, already knowing the answer. It's because I didn't want to face what I'd see when I did open my eyes.

Sweat trickled down my neck and was instantly cooled by a breeze. My window was open, and I could hear the faint sounds of street traffic below. Why was it so hot as opposed to the cold I remembered? It was winter after all. My least favorite season.

And why was mama here? It couldn't be anything good if she was nearby.

Had I gotten drunk, came home, and passed out? Oh shit, she was *really* going to let me have it then. I had promised her I'd never do it again.

From the time I can remember, whenever I had fucked up I woke up to her hovering over me. Or laying down next to me or sitting in a chair by my bed. Either way she was there when I woke up. What followed was a variety of things. A spanking when I was younger over whatever I did, erratic crying over whatever I did, arguing and yelling over whatever I did, swearing and throwing shit around my room over whatever I did. And she always did it with love.

God, let me just stay asleep. Don't wake up Jayd. Stay asleep. Forever, if you can.

Ignoring my thoughts, I began to open my eyes. Fuck it. Just face whatever you did. You won't have to live here much longer.

I slowly pried my eyes open. It was such a struggle. They felt crusted, or glued shut. How strange. That had never happened before. With all the strength I could muster in my body I tore my eyelids open.

Ouch.

"Augghh!" I bemoaned.

I don't know what hurt more. The pain of my crusted eyelids ripping open or the bright lights that stabbed my vision as soon as my eyes adjusted. I immediately closed my eyes again, but not before getting a glimpse of Mama springing up from a chair that sat beside my bed.

Oh, and Molly's annoying ass standing in the corner looking over at me. Why did she have to always be near?

"Jayd!?" Mama exclaimed. I felt her move over towards me and her figure stood right above me.

"Ugh...Hi mom" I said, not sounding pleased to be talking to her at all. I spoke in the driest croaking I've ever heard me speak. Minor stabs of pain coasted the back of my throat. How much did I drink??

"Jayd!?" Mama said again. "You're awake? Oh my God! Thank you Jesus!"

What? Why did she sound so relieved? So frantic?

"Opal!?" Mama shouted. "Opal, get in here! Jayd's up! She's awake!"

Opal? Aunt Opal was here? What the hell...why?

The sound of thundering steps pounded the floor as someone ran up the main hall and towards my room. My bedroom door burst open soon after.

"What?!" a familiar voice gasped. I could recognize that voice in a sea of conversations. Aunt Opal was loud, crass, and had the typical rough smoker voice, but with a hint of southern twang in a unique tone. I actually liked it, though I did not like her at all.

But, why was she here? Last she had said, she was moving to the Caribbean with a new Trinidadian guy that she had recently met.

"Jayd?!" Aunt Opal yelled.

Yes? What was it?

"Jayd?!" Mama yelled.

Yes? For fuck sake, what?

"Jayd," Mama whispered. "Aww, baby, you're alive. You're alive. We didn't think you'd wake up again."

Um...Excuse Me…?

Chapter 1

"You make any of those calls yet, Jayd?," Aunt Opal asked me as I poured some frosted mini wheats into a bowl. Sitting the box of cereal down I reached for the milk. I slowly poured and began to hum. Soft fur brushed up against my leg, followed by low purring. Our cat Norman was hungry. I glanced down quickly at the all-black feline and made a quick kissy face at him. A large set of orange-yellow eyes stared back up at me.

Molly stood in the corner silent, smiling.

"Jayd, did you hear me?", my aunt asked.

I had my back to her, standing at the counter in our tiny apartment kitchen. I watched the milk flow out of the plastic carton and into my bowl, flowing over each piece of cereal. Drowning them.

"Jayd?" my aunt said again in an aggravated tone. "Now I know you hear me, girl!"

Yes, I do. But it's none of your fucking business, Auntie Opal. Go feed Norman or find something else to do other than bother me.

Go on Jayd, answer your aunt.

Molly spoke to me in her usual irritating statements. She never moved her lips, but I could always hear what she said and feel her presence even when she wasn't in full view.

I stopped pouring the milk and sat the carton down. Giving a soft sign and relaxing my shoulders, I mumbled out an answer.

"No, Aunt Opal. I haven't".

"And why not?" she shot back.

Putting the lid back on the carton of milk, I dug into the drawer under the sink where we kept our silverware. I fetched a spoon and plopped it into my cereal. Norman was now under the table, pawing at my aunt's ankle. Grabbing my bowl, I swirled around and headed towards my sanctuary. Also known as my bedroom.

I could feel Molly following from behind.

"And where do you think you're going?" My Aunt Opal asked. "Food is to be eaten at the kitchen table, not in your room".

Molly snickered.

I stopped in my tracks and whirled around. At times like this I wished I was invisible.

Who am I kidding? I always wished I was invisible.

I marched over to the kitchen table where my aunt was and sat down across from her with my bowl of cereal. Hunching over the bowl I gobbled down each spoon full and swallowed as fast as I could. The quicker I finished, the quicker I could get out of here.

Streams of sunlight drifted through the kitchen window, and from my view, a bright blue sky hovered above with not a single cloud in sight. It was a beautiful day outside, and I wanted to go for a walk and get some air. Get the hell out of this stuffy ass apartment.

"And you didn't answer me," Aunt Opal continued, picking Norman up and caressing him in her arms. He purred and rubbed himself up against her chest. "Why haven't you called any of those people yet, Jayd?"

Yeah Jayd, why haven't you called any of those people yet? Molly stood beside me, peering down. Grinning.

"Shut up, Molly!" I muttered under my breath, and quickly regretted it.

"Excuse me...what...?!" Aunt Opal cried.

Aunt Opal was talking about the list of psychiatrists that was given and suggested to me by my doctor last week when I went in for my first check up after waking up. Dr. Martinez, my long time physician, had wanted me to look into getting someone to talk to.

Actually, it was more like he demanded I find one, and even let my mom and aunt know how important it was that I talk to someone.

"You're lucky to be alive, Jayd. Take this opportunity to speak to someone and heal. Do it for your mom and aunt." He hesitated. "And if that isn't enough, do it for her. Do it for that woman."

It hurt when he said that. No. Not hurt. Hurt was too mild of a feeling. As I stood there listening to his pleas, his words were tearing me apart. Her. That woman.

She had a name, and ever since I woke up from my months long coma and heard her name, it never stopped echoing in my mind. When I slept, when I ate, showered, and drank. And when I laid in bed crying for hours. She had a name but it was a name that I was unsuccessfully trying to push into the distance of my memory. I want to archive her name and only bring it forth when I am ready to face it.

But people never gave me a fucking chance to. It didn't matter that I was still recovering. It didn't matter that I needed to heal first, to breathe, to accept. None of that mattered because of what happened. It was always brought up. No one had to say anything really. I could feel it in the air when I walked by familiar faces. The quick glimpses and side eyes. The whispering, the staring, the head shaking, the astonishment of it all. And the...hatred?

No, I didn't have a chance. Not even on the first day when I woke up. I was told everything. Everything that they thought mattered.

It mattered that I had tried to kill myself by jumping off of the Brooklyn Bridge and that a woman jumped in after me to try and save me and... and...

"Nothing," I told Aunt Opal. "I was just talking to myself."

Aunt Opal glared at me. Molly smirked.

"Jayd, I'll ask you again!" my aunt bellowed. She was always so loud. Why was she always so loud?

"Why haven't you called any of the people Dr. Martinez gave you?"

"I am!" I told her, my voice rising. "I'm going to do it today!".

Aunt Opal leaned back against the kitchen chair she sat in, her head cocked to the side and eyes wide. Her lips formed a frown and she slowly crossed her arms across her chest.

Here we go. You've done it now, Jayd.

"Who the hell do you think you-", she began shouting, just as mama came through the door.

Mama walked backwards with a basket of laundry in her arms. She turned around to face us as Aunt Opal and I watched her.

She wore a bright yellow short-sleeved t-shirt, ripped blue jeans, and white sneakers. Her light brown hair was tied into a high bun with a yellow handkerchief. Her milk chocolate skin glistened, and when she smiled, the whole room lit up. She looked like a teenager, despite almost being 40.

Mama sat the basket of clothes on the floor, dusted off her hands, and looked up at us.

"What's all this racket in here?" she asked in her sweet southern drawl. "I could hear you both from downstairs in the laundry room!"

Aunt Opal and I stared at her. My mother was beautiful. No, not just beautiful. Beautiful was too simple. She looked so young and innocent. Her movements were graceful and she had a skip in her every step. Her voice was like sweet tea, and she had a charming and dreamy far away look in her eyes. Like an adorable lost kitten.

I resembled her quite a bit, but less charming and alluring. Mama said I was a mysterious and withdrawn version of herself.

Aunt Opal said I looked nothing like Mama. Not even in my wildest delusions.

I could see why my father, and many men before him, fell for Mama. It was too bad her beauty wasn't enough to make my father stick around. The piece of shit left before I was born. Lucky me. I never had, nor would even want to meet him.

Mama, whose name was Ruby Broussard, was the fairest of the three Broussard sisters from New Orleans. Opal Broussard was the oldest, Pearl Broussard the middle daughter, and Ruby the youngest. Twenty years ago they all moved here to Harlem, New York, and occasionally would go back home to visit. My Aunt Pearl had since moved to Florida.

Aunt Opal answered her.

"*Your* child" she sneered, "Over here, hasn't gone to any appointments yet and has the nerve to sass mouth me!"

Mama crossed her arms and looked at me. Her pretty brown eyes darkened.

"Jayd, is that true?" she asked. Although her eyes were hard, her voice was still soft.

"No!" I refuted. "She asked, and I just told her that I was going to one today."

"So I'm a liar?" Aunt Opal shot back.

My head was beginning to throb. I honestly couldn't stand Aunt Opal. I despised her. Ever since I was little, it always seemed like she had something against me. What that was, I never could tell. But I always speculated it was because I had stolen my mother's attention away from her the day I was born.

You see, when they were younger, Mama used to worship Aunt Opal and follow her around like a puppy. She was the cool, big sister to her younger, pretty, charming, little sister. Aunt Opal was a big talker and ambitious. She often talked shit, but had the backbone to defend it. The scars on her face told the story of a rough, brolic, woman who got into one too many fights in her heyday. Aunt Opal wasn't ugly, but she sure wasn't pretty in any sense of the word.

She had broad shoulders and asymmetrical features. Her skin was a lovely shade of mahogany and she had a nice height on her. But, she wasn't slender or graceful, although she had a nice shape. Her eyes were beady and harsh, perhaps from years of disappointment, from family members, to the men in her life, and to acquaintances. Aunt Opal was also beginning to bald in front of her hairline and her lips were black from all the smoking over the years. Added to that, her constant rudeness and hostility she gave off, gained her no fans or friends among people.

But Mama always looked up to Aunt Opal as her protector and rock against hard times. After all, it was Aunt Opal there to defend her against the schoolyard bullies, and Aunt Opal to cuss out the cat calling young men who stalked Mama in her youth. It was Aunt Opal who held the family together when my Granddaddy died leaving the family in financial distress, when she took on multiple jobs to support her family. It was also Aunt Opal's shoulder that Mama cried on when my sperm donor took off after she told him she was pregnant. Mama had followed Aunt Opal to Harlem and Aunt Opal was the breadwinner for a long time until recently. Mama stayed home.

Despite this, Aunt Opal never received her due in the presence of Mama. Mama was just that enchanting and she could never do no wrong. Mama was Granny's favorite, even up until the day she passed, it was Mama who she wanted by her side. It was Mama who men flocked to and women kissed up to and people held doors open for or got out of their seats for.

In truth, I felt sorry for Aunt Opal. I admired her strength and pride. But I felt that I had taken the attention of the one person that looked up to her in awe the way the world looked up at her sister.

"Look," I exasperated, turning to my aunt. "I'm sorry, okay, I'm going today. I made an appointment with a Dr. Ca-Corrandy."

I got up from the table, picked up my now empty bowl, and headed for the sink. My aunt and mother watched me. I needed to get out of this apartment. It was too stuffy and hot in here and this tiny, old, kitchen made it worse. This tiny hideously lime green painted kitchen. What was Mama thinking when she painted it?

Before either could say a word, I dropped my bowl and spoon into the sink, kissed Mama on the cheek goodbye, and headed down the hall out the front door. On my way out I could hear them conversing, with Aunt Opal's loud mouth thundering over Mama's.

"Ruby, you betta get that crazy child some help!" she told Mama. "Before they end up putting her away for good! There's something seriously wrong with her!"

Mama's voice echoed down the hall.

"Opal, c'mon. You know how sensitive Jayd always is."

Chapter 2

Jayd.

My name. Like the gemstone.

Pronounced the exact way it's spelled. I always thought it was missing an e on the end. Mama liked the unique spelling of it, she had told the nurse after my delivery.

My grandmother had named all of her daughters after jewels, so Mama thought she'd keep the tradition going by naming me after one.

But why not Jade? The normal way it should be spelled. It never made sense to me and it never looked right. I remember asking Mama about it when I was little.

"Cause it's unique, baby!" she had told me, while endearingly pinching my nose. "Just like you!"

Dr. Corrandy, the psychiatrist that sat in front of me, thought so as well.

"Jayd...that's a unique spelling of the name. Never seen it spelled like that before."

I nodded at him in response but kept my mouth closed. I made good on my promise today to see one of the psychiatrists given to me by Dr. Martinez, but I had no intention of opening up to any of them.

Dr. Corrandy was a middle aged White man with thick glasses and already balding, gray hair. He wore a well tailored suit, as if he were a businessman not a psychiatrist.

I wore a simple white t-shirt, new white sneakers, a jean jacket, and blue jeans.

White sneakers walking around New York. I must indeed be crazy.

I sat across from him at his desk in his spacious office. What threw me completely off was that the objects and furniture around the room were all unusually circular. The coffee table to the right of us. A perfect circle. The chairs, desks, a vase, the front door. Even the windows were circles. The uneasy churning of my stomach began to spin, as it was all clearly done on purpose. I wonder why though?

"So, Jayd," Dr. Corrandy began "How have you been feeling since the... accident?"

He hesitated to call it an accident instead of what it truly was. A suicide attempt. They all hesitated. Mama and Aunt Opal. Dr. Martinez and Aunt Pearl on the phone. They all called it an accident. Like I merely knocked over a glass or tripped over a rock.

Like I didn't mean to hurl myself over the bridge that day.

Molly leaned against the circular window behind Dr. Corrandy's desk. Her arms crossed, and that same smug smirk on her face as the one earlier in the kitchen. She wore her usual white sundress and white sneakers and her messy hair tied into a bun. She looked like nineteen-year-old present day me, but dressed like a little nine-year old me. I guess if I thought about it, it all made sense why she appeared that way.

Molly caught me looking at her and stuck out her tongue. I quickly averted my gaze back at Dr. Corrandy.

"I've been…" I pondered how to answer this question.

After some thought, I told him the truth.

"I don't know how I feel, Dr. Corrandy"

"Hmm…" He nodded.

"Perhaps you've been repressing your thoughts and emotions since the accident. I've read up on your case and Dr. Martinez and I discussed a bit about you before your visit today. I don't doubt that you do not want to relive what happened that day. The pain, anger, and the...guilt you must feel about it all."

Ugh.

Why is Dr. Corrandy so typical of a psychiatrist? I half expected him to pull out a chaise lounge couch, a note pad, and ask me to lay down and say *"So how does it make you feel?"*

And why didn't he just come out and say it? Am I repressing my emotions because I feel guilty about…*her*?

"That young woman...who lost her life," Dr. Corrandy shuffled uncomfortably in his seat. A chill could be felt in the air even though it was nearing the summer season and the windows were shut. I wanted to just get up and leave. To fly out of this chair, out of this office, out of this building, and home to my bedroom. My stuffed, cramped bedroom.
Or to Pat's Room down the street from our apartment to have a beer.

Or wine, or Vodka. Something. Anything to drown out and make me forget today.

"What are you looking at Jayd?" Dr. Corrandy asked. He turned his head around to see what was behind him. He of course saw nothing.

Should I tell him about Molly?

No. I shouldn't do that. I shouldn't *ever* tell anyone about Molly. It was bad enough they thought I was a depressive manic, but to tell them about someone that only I could see would be disastrous. They'd have no choice but to put me away. For good.

And besides. I didn't like nor trust Dr. Corrandy enough to let him in.

I watched him. Examined every angle and corner of his face. Analyzed his features and expression. His clothes and his desk. Even his fingernails.

What an unattractive and exhausted looking man. His eyes were hooded and worry lines were stretched across his white face. He was also severely balding in the middle of his head.

A suit that was a little too tight and too dressed up for this occasion. Glasses that hung on the bridge of his hooked nose that were desperately in need of being tightened. No wedding ring present on his finger. And where his nails...bitten?

"Ms. Broussard, are you alright?" Dr. Corrandy asked. My eyes wandered to my hands sitting on my lap. Small, dainty, and scarred.

"Yes...no..." My head hung down as I responded. Not because I was intimated or embarrassed, but because I needed to focus on something else before I broke down.

"Jayd...I need you to answer me," he said. I could feel his eyes on me. Those heavy, hooded eyes.

"Jayd, I need you to look at me?" he spoke again. My head lifted until our eyes met. I sucked in my breath. Crow's feet lined his eyes. Why hadn't I noticed before? I wonder if it was from frowning. I didn't see any frown lines. Maybe it was from smiling and laughing. I didn't think Dr. Corrandy was the type to smile or laugh very often. But his eyes...

His eyes were clear and sympathetic. I didn't notice it before. I wonder why he got into this mental health profession? Was he caring? Or just curious?

I often wondered why people become psychiatrists? Who would voluntarily take on the emotions and pain of another? Were us patients a piece of a puzzle that had to be put back into place and become a good citizen in society? Or were we the puzzles with the missing pieces that needed to be found. To make us whole again? Sane again? Normal again?

Why wasn't Dr. Corrandy married? Certificates lined the walls of his office. Did he devote too much of his time to his craft and neglect his personal life? Why was he balding so badly? Was he stressed out? Why take on such a commitment to the point of being stressed? Maybe he saw himself as a martyr or a hero?
I shouldn't judge him. I shouldn't judge anyone. I was in no place to *ever* judge anyone. No. Not me. Least of all me.

"Jayd…" Dr. Corrandy said softly. There wasn't an ounce of annoyance in his voice. He sounded...patient.

"Jayd...I want you to talk to me. What are you thinking?" Such a soft voice. He blinked his eyes. My head began to hang down as I prepared to look down at my hands again.

Had I been staring the whole time at him? How awkward.

"Are you thinking about Melanie, Jayd?" he asked.

My head shot up like a bullet. My mouth whipped open like a switch.

"No!" I shouted. I didn't mean to shout. Now he definitely will think I'm lying.

His eyes narrowed and his lips pursed. It was so quiet in the room that I could almost hear both of our hearts beating. Outside, the sky was darkening. The wind was picking up and the birds were chirping wildly. A storm was coming. And I no longer wanted to be in this building or in this room with this man. I stood up.

"I'm not feeling well, Sir. I think I'm going to go home now."

Dr. Corrandy didn't respond, except he sat still with the same expression on his face as if he were in deep thought. I watched him as his eyes followed me and I turned to pick up my things and headed for the door.

I was nearly half way across the room before I heard him speak.

"You know Jayd, suppressing the past and what happened isn't going to make it go away. What happened was real. It was tragic and unnecessary."

I stopped in my tracks and stood still, listening to him.

"You tried to relieve yourself of hurt, and did it in a way that was selfish to those around you. Someone showed you kindness that day and paid for it with their life. Now others are hurting. Your actions had terrible consequences, and you can't run away from them forever."

I'm not running away from anything, you bastard. Shut up.

Molly stood in front of the door, leaning on it. Blocking my exit. She mouthed Dr. Corrandy's words.

"Owning up to what you did is the only way forward. You'll never find your peace of mind until you do, Jayd."

I could hear my heartbeat slamming against my ribcage as it ramped up. My eyes were watering and my fist were tightly clenched against my sides. The unusual room of circles felt as though they were steadily closing in. I grabbed my bag tightly around the strap.

"Melanie. I read about your case and what happened. The woman's name was Melanie. I know you think about her and about what happened that day."

Shut up.
Just shut the fuck up. What do you know?

"The guilt must be eating at you, Jayd. The regret. Knowing that it was because of you. Because you-"

And like that, the bag around my shoulder leaped out of my hand and flew across the room, smacking the psychiatrist right in the head.

Molly's giddy laughter erupted throughout the room.

Chapter 3

"Please tell Dr. Corrandy that I'm extremely sorry and embarrassed," Mama soft voice drifted throughout my bedroom. "I don't know what she was thinking. Yes. Yes. Thank you so much Miss!" Mama said into her cell phone as she stood at the foot of my bed.

I watched her hang up as I sat on my bed with my knees pressed against my stomach, waiting for the eruption that was coming next.

Mama threw her phone onto my bed and looked at me, dead in the eyes. She crossed her arms and glared at me with those beautiful almond-shaped eyes of hers. Her foot began tapping.
When Mama's foot tapped, that's when I knew I was really in trouble.

"Jayd!" she bellowed. "What the hell is wrong with you?!"

I struggled to speak. I knew I should just be quiet as I really didn't have any reasonings nor justifications. "I...I..."

"What were you thinking about attacking Dr. Corrandy?" she asked.

"I didn't attack him..." I mumbled.

Yeah, but you nearly knocked him out with your bag!

I could hear Molly next to me, but I couldn't see her.

"You hit him with your bag Jayd" Mama yelled. "The poor man's receptionist said he has a knot the size of a golf ball!"

Heehee

Shut up, Molly.

"Well?!" Mama asked. She wanted an answer and I knew she wouldn't leave until she got one.

"You're extremely lucky he's not pressing charges! He doesn't want you back and has dropped you as a patient!

Good. I wasn't planning on seeing that man again. If I did, he'd end up with two golf-size knots.

But anyway, I couldn't tell Mama the real reason I hit Dr. Corrandy in the face with my bag.
That he was condescending and insincere. That he was the type of person that wouldn't listen even if I did speak. That he had other motives for wanting me to speak.

That he indirectly shamed and blamed me for something that I wasn't ready to come to terms with.

My throat tightened, but I simply responded in the best way I knew how.

"I'm sorry Mama. I lost my cool. Tell Dr. Corrandy that I apologize and please excuse my behavior."

"Tell him yourself Jayd!" She shifted from one foot to the other with her arms still crossed. "I don't know what's happening with you! I thought you were getting better. Making progress. You've been acting strange lately!"
"Hmph," came a noise at the door, but I paid it no attention.

I knew Aunt Opal was standing in the doorway being noisy and listening to me and Mama. I knew she was enjoying the entire thing. She would never miss a moment when I was being scolded by Mama. She enjoyed me being miserable. I didn't even turn in her direction.

My head hurt, and as much as I loved Mama, I wanted her to shut up and get out of my room so that I could lay down. So I decided to become agreeable.

"I'll call Dr. Corrandy tomorrow and apologize," was all I said.

I could feel her eyes on me. Studying me, and still very much enraged. She was expecting me to say more but I was now looking down at my badly bitten fingernails.

When it became apparent that I wasn't going to say more, Mama huffed and turned towards the door.

"You had better let him know how sorry you are and that you're thankful that he isn't pursuing legal action! Girl, if you were still a child, I'd spank you to the bone shown through!" she said, with hints of a dwindling southern accent.

"And start looking for another psychiatrist! Whether you like it or not, as long as you live under my roof, you will get help and show that you have some manners! You can't just keep pushing people away, Jayd!"

Before walking out, Mama turned back to me. "I want you to find a job as well, Jayd. No more sitting up in this room all day. Get up and go out and look for a job. It'll be something that you can do before you start school in the fall. If you need help with filling out applications let me know."

She left and I turned to watch her go. Aunt Opal stood watching in glee as Mama brushed past her. I flopped down on the side of my bed with my arm dangling over. Aunt Opal snickered before shutting my door.

Empty silence filled the room. Like the calm after the storm. I was breathing deeply and slowly when a voice rang out in my head.

Ugh, what a bitch.

It was Molly. She had made her presence fully known as I tilted my head up and watched as she walked to and sat at the end of my bed. I laid back down, shielding my eyes with an arm as the other one lay hanging. I could feel Molly's eyes on me. Anticipation radiated off of her. She, like Mama and Dr. Corrandy, expected me to say something.

When will they learn?

My hanging hand tickled as I felt fur lightly brush against it. Soft purrs accompanied by a meow and a gentle lick of my arm.

I looked down to see Norman, who must've sneaked in during all the commotion and hid under my bed. I quickly sat up and gathered him into my arms, pressing my face against his head and body against my chest. He radiated with purrs.

We, or rather I, had found Norman as a kitten when I was six. I heard little mews coming from around the back of our apartment near the dumpster. I had been playing outside and those were the days when I was still innocent of the ills of the world and was just a young carefree little girl.

When I heard the little mews, I stopped playing and sought out the source of the noise. The other kids that I had been playing with had followed me to see what I was up to. As I inched towards one of the dumpsters, the sounds got louder. When I could clearly make out the mews, I knew instantly what was making the noise, and I raced around to the back of a dumpster only to find nothing.

It smelled horrible, even worse than what usual garbage was supposed to smell like. The kids that had followed me began to complain and gag, but they too heard the noise and had begun to search.

I continued to hear the little mews, but I had no idea where it was coming from. They were loud, stressed, and panicked. Where were the kittens?

I searched the entire area around the dumpsters and still found nothing. By now, the mews were consistent and very frantic. I stood there for a moment in confusion before the painful truth hit me. I didn't want to believe it as a naive six year old, but my body knew. My legs moved towards the dumpster where I first heard the mews before my mind could accept it.

"Hey!" I shouted to the other kids. "Help me up!"

One of the boys lifted me up and I cautiously opened the lid. The powerful odor of death hit me. Some of the kids screamed and a few began to run away.

"Oh my God!" I shouted.

On top of the piles of garbage bags lay 4 kittens. I knew three were dead as flies flew around them and they laid there stiff and unmoving. One of the kittens had been crying out in terror. It was on top of its siblings and shrieking as flies swarmed around. The kitten was all black and its eyes weren't even. I would later learn that it was only about a week old. I picked the kitten up and cradled it as I ran home.

Both Mama and Aunt Opal told me absolutely not, ain't no cat coming in here.

I cried and whined, but they didn't care.

Hopping and throwing myself around on the floor and couch, I was hysterical. I told them that he was all alone and that his siblings were all dead. That the kitten was alone in this world and that it would die as well if we didn't help it. When I showed Mama the kitten she gasped and quickly took it away from me.

"I don't care!" Aunt Opal had bellowed. "Does this look like an animal shelter to you?"

I ignored her and followed Mama into the bathroom as she put the kitten into the bathtub and began to run warm water.

"Go get me a towel!" she instructed and I ran to get one. Aunt Opal sucked her teeth and leaned into the bathroom.

"Ruby, don't let that cat in here! Look how dirty it is! It could be diseased! " You're a disease, I had said to myself. It was the first time I had truly decided that I hated Aunt Opal.

"Opal, it's just a baby! Eyes aren't even open!" Mama told her.

I pushed past Aunt Opal in the doorway and handed Mama a towel.

Mama told Aunt Opal to go buy kitten formula, and Aunt Opal, disgruntled, left to do so.

I had always found it funny how Mama managed to boss Aunt Opal around and still does to this day, despite being the youngest one.

Me and Mama spent the rest of the day cleaning and feeding the kitten. The next day we took it to the vet and was told that the kitten was no more than a week and a half old when it had been thrown out like trash and abandoned along with its siblings. The kitten was male, and was suffering from severe malnourishment and would need to stay in intensive care. The vet had told my mom that it was unlikely the kitten would live.

"And don't you go crying either if it dies!" Aunt Opal had told me. Mama wrapped her arm around me and pulled me in close.

As the days went by, I prayed for the kitten to live. I had even come up with a name for him; Norman, after my maternal grandfather.

With each passing day I was becoming more and more depressed. At six, I already was painfully aware that there were evil people in the world. I had been told my daddy was one of them. I had been made aware that it was those that would harm the weak, the innocent, and the defenseless. Never stray too far off from the apartment, Mama would always say.

I barely ate and did not go outside to play. Mama was worried about me and Aunt Opal just rolled her eyes.

"All this over a cat!" she sneered.

Three weeks passed and one day I heard Mama coming up the hallway stairs from work as I sat in the living room watching cartoons.

I swung around ready to greet her when I was met with a fluffy, Black, orangey-yellow-eyed kitten in her arms. I shrieked loudly, enough to wake up Aunt Opal from her nap in her room, and ran around the couch to grip the kitten in my arms. I pressed him close and dug my face into his fur. He didn't resist and his demeanor was sweet as he mewed and licked me.

Mama smiled as I walked to the couch and cuddled Norman, Aunt Opal ran into the room and then rolled her eyes and sucked her teeth when she saw what I was holding.

I didn't get many Christmas presents that year, because Norman's care at the vet had been expensive, but I had gotten something so much better. Norman was thirteen now, and a black fluff ball. With his yellow-orange eyes, and pitch-black fur, he reminded me of Halloween.

One that day he was brought home, six-year-old me had said something that I believe still haunts the three of us till this day.

"Norman!" I cried cuddling him. "I'm so glad you're alive! I wouldn't have wanted to live if I had found out you died too!"

Mama then stopped smiling and Aunt Opal's eyes widened.

Norman was my only comfort in this apartment. I remember seeing him hop up and lay next to me the day I woke up from my coma after the...accident.

He never left my side until it was time to eat. Then he'd be back; looking up at me with those oversized orange-yellow eyes. Now here he was again, looking up at me in my arms.

I wonder if he, too, was waiting for me to say something.

I laid back onto my bed and let Norman roll up into a ball and nap beside me.

Reaching down and searching, I found my hidden stash of vodka tucked on top of the wooden slabs under my bed. With my other hand, I reached for my antidepressants on the other side of my bed sitting on a night stand.

Isn't that something? The closest people to me in this world were my Mama and a cat.
I guess being a bit above average and a girl had aided in people not writing me off as a complete fucking weirdo.

I popped a few capsules and downed them with vodka. I'm running low on my supply.

I think I'll go to Pat's Room later today for a few shots and see if he could offer me a few bottles at a discount.

Shit. I forgot.
I'm broke.

Chapter 4

"Yes? Yes? Come in!" the tiny, middle aged, Italian woman gestured towards me from behind the counter as I stopped outside of a small antique shop and rang the bell. I could see that she had a mustache and a large mole on her nose as she turned to me to speak.

I hurried inside and was met with a strong smell of incense and garlic. Walking to the counter, I titled over slightly so that the woman could see and hear me clearly. I wasn't even sure she was at least 4 feet tall. She sat on a stool and had been flicking through a magazine. On the counter sat a bowl of soup and a large piece of garlic bread.

Taking Mama's advice, or more like her command, I went job hunting today. Roaming the streets of Harlem, the rhythmic sounds of honking cars, people shouting everywhere, and the smells, both good and bad filled the air. The shrieks of children crying and laughing, women gossiping and men hustling flowed all around me. I had passed by and popped into many stores and institutions to ask about employment, but hadn't had any success. My online applications weren't getting me anywhere and I was growing frustrated.

It wasn't until I passed by this tiny antique shop and had nearly missed a *Help Wanted* sign written on beaten up cardboard in cursive writing that I had finally gotten lucky.

Now I stood in front of this tiny, unusual looking woman and began to question her about the sign outside.

"Good afternoon, Ma'am. There's a sign outside your shop that says Help Wanted. I'm looking for employment."

The tiny woman peered up at me and then immediately looked back down at her magazine.

"Yes. I need someone to sweep up around here. Wash the windows and shelves I cannot reach, and mind the store when I'm gone."

I struggled to keep a laugh inside.

Poor lady, it must be a struggle to be that short.

At least she's seeking help for her problems...unlike someone we know...

Of course Molly was here. She couldn't help but follow me everywhere now, especially since the incident.

My eyes wandered around the shop and fell on several antiques that I found rather interesting. Several old chairs and lamps lined against a wall. Vases, pottery, candles, and what looked to be a giant lyre sat to the right of me. Tall shelves were spaced out around the room. I could see the dust on antiques and shelves alike. Unopened boxes were also stacked around the shop. I spotted a door at the back and another door to the left of it, possibly a storage room. I didn't see any bathroom. This place was super cluttered and dusty. On top of that the smells of incense and garlic was making me queasy.

"You will need to be here at eight a.m. in the morning to look after the store until twelve p.m." the woman said. "I will come by to check on everything and you can have a break during that hour. Be back here by one p.m. and do some dusting and cleaning. Answer calls to the shop and service customers as they come in. You can then leave at four or five p.m. By then, I should be able to take over until midnight. My name is Sylvia, and you can call me such."

Before I could get a word in, she continued on.

"Any lateness or missed day, you are immediately fired. I had trouble with the last girl about this. I will not tolerate it! I am running a business here and my work and reputation will not be damaged by some incompetent, lazy girls!"

My eyes wandered over Sylvia's face, her neck, and then her tiny body. Her voice and tone were loud and overbearing, but her body language told a different story. Chest pushed forward with a pout on her lips with hands on her hips and glaring eyes. She was trying to appear opposing and intimidating the way a child would to an adult who would only find it entertaining. I suddenly felt sad for her. In life, she most likely always had to be loud and stern if she wanted people to attempt to take her seriously due to her height and size. I bet she always comes off as cold and irrational to people, only because they didn't see what she truly felt like inside. Small and invisible in the big, wide world. I wondered if she was married.

"You will be paid fifteen dollars an hour for your work. Now, is all of this clear to you, young lady?"

"Yes...ma'am," I replied. It was a decent salary and on top of it, it appeared I would be alone and unbothered working here. I didn't like the idea of working at an office. Never did. It didn't suit me at all to be micromanaged by my employer, or forced to engage with co-workers that I couldn't care less about and who probably didn't like me anyway.

Nope. This job would be perfect. I could already tell people hardly came in here, as the shop was easy to miss and was full of dust and cobwebs. Even the dusty register looked like it hadn't been opened in years.

"Um, ma'am. Is there a restroom here?" I tentatively asked.

"No! You'll have to go out and find one. And don't eat in here either. There are already enough bugs here and the food attracts them!"

I looked down at the bowl of soup and piece of garlic bread on the counter. Sylvia noticed this.

"Hey missy!" she exclaimed. "This is *my* shop. It's been in my family and I've worked here for thirty years. I'll damn eat in here if I want!"

She sat back in her stool and began reading her magazine. It was a large magazine and I could no longer see her as it completely engulfed her.

"Come back tomorrow. You can start then. Remember to be here by 8 a.m., or don't bother coming at all."

As she spoke, I found myself tuning out. I often did whenever people yelled or were crass with me. Block them out like a cloud blocking out the sun.

My eyes drifted around to an odd-looking antique that sat on the shelf to my right. A brightly tinted copper and wooden dove figurine stood neatly on the shelf. The dove was elegantly designed and had a round gap in its back. It took me a while to realize that it was used to prop something up. But what? Flowers? Candles?

The dove was both vintage and unique. I loved it.

The figurine drew me in as I continued to peer at it longer than I should as I heard a stern grunt from below me. I looked down to see Sylvia watching me, her arms crossed and a frown on her face.

"Uh, sorry Ma'am! I was just looking at that dove statue. It's beautiful." I said, stuttering from embarrassment. I hope she didn't think I would try to steal it.

"Never you mind about the statue! All of my antiques are beautiful, I wouldn't allow anything less in my shop! You will need to clean them all."

I quickly glanced around and found Sylvia to be right. Despite many being dusty and worn, the antiques in the store were stunning. It looked almost as if I was in a museum gazing at artifacts. Abet, a tiny, cluttered, and dusty museum. I was really going to enjoy looking at these all day. I bet each artifact told a story. I turned back to Sylvia.

"I'll be here tomorrow at eight a.m."

I walked out of the shop and headed home. Well, lucky me. Now maybe Mama and Aunt Opal would get off of my back and stop nagging me about laying around. Even as a child, I loved history so working at an antique shop was quite fitting. I could feel Molly's presence trailing behind me.

Cars roared past me on the street and a little boy on a scooter shot by in a hurry, nearly tripping himself.
Melanie...

I wonder if Melanie liked antiques. What was her favorite subject in school when she was younger? She looked like the type of girl who would have been great at all subjects. And popular with other students.

Melanie…

The news article said she was looking forward to getting married later this year. A September wedding, her fian had said. Martha Vineyard. Lilacs and lilies. Champagne and a white wedding dress. Every girl's dream.

And I destroyed that dream for one of them.

Ringggggg

The sound of my cell phone made me jump. Pulling it out of my pocket, I looked to see who was calling. It was Mama.

"Yeah, Mama?" I said as I put the phone to my ear.

"Jayd! Dr. Corrandy has found another therapist for you. Thank the Lord! A woman this time. She's...Black American too I believe. Dr. Corrandy said it might be for the best that you speak to someone who you could maybe relate to."

Of course he did. It couldn't be the fact that he was an asshole was the reason he got knocked in the head. No, it was definitely because he wasn't 'relatable'. Now I definitely wasn't apologizing to him.
"Jayd please go to her! I'm worried about you, baby!" Mama pleaded on the other end.

"Ok, Mama. I'll go to her" I said to her.

I didn't need convincing. I could deal with Mama being mad, but couldn't handle her being sad or worried. Especially about me.

"Good!" she said.

"I found a job! Pays fifteen dollars an hour. It's at an antique shop. I start tomorrow at eight." I told her, hoping to cheer her up with the news.

She lit up like a light bulb.

"That's good, baby!" Mama exclaimed. "See what I told you? Just keep looking and you'll find one. Now get home. I'm making chicken gumbo tonight and need help in the kitchen."

Yum.

Chapter 5

I sat staring at a thick slab of neck meat from behind. Pat was hunched over and pulling wine glasses out of the lower bottle shelf of his bar. He was severely perspiring and I could smell him from across the room where I was laying down on his couch. But I wouldn't have rather been anywhere else.

Guzzling down a light spritzer, I closed my eyes and listened to the music. A mixture of vintage music from the sixties and seventies drifted throughout the room. I hummed along to the choruses.

Pat wouldn't let me have any more vodka shots. He told me that I needed to take a break or I'd end up passed out in a gutter and he'd end up in jail when it was discovered that he was selling alcohol to a minor.

"All right! That's it. Fucking finally!" I heard him say over the noise, as he slammed the cabinet shelf door shut. I sat up.

"It was barely two boxes full, Pat." I mocked him.

"Shut the hell up! I don't see you helping! Just sitting your lazy ass down on my couch!" he shot back. "These glasses cost me over four hundred dollars! And they're heavy as fuck!"

"You could use the exercise," I told him.

Pat swiftly glanced over at me and grunted.

"You're growing a little beer belly yourself, sweetheart." he said, motioning at my stomach with his hand.

And he was right. Mama saw it too and remarked on how I must be sneaking extra plates of dinner when she wasn't around.

Pat was as thick as he was wide. He bounced when he walked, and I found it humorous. He was a pale-skinned Puerto Rican with reddish-brown hair and black eyes. He was stocky, stout, very fat, short; and I was a few feet taller than him. He was nowhere near as short as Sylvia though.

He bent down again to open the cabinet shelf.

"Aaargh! Seventy-eight glasses and all for what? Because two shit-heads couldn't keep their fucking brawls outta my bar!"

He was talking about some incident that happened a few days back. Two guys got into an argument and began throwing glasses, breaking chairs, and swinging fists. They were permanently banned. I was happy as hell. This was the one place other than my room that I considered a second sanctuary and I didn't want idiots ruining it.

I watched as he shut the cabinet shelf shut and went into the backroom. My eyes quickly glanced around the room, taking in everything that I had to get used to again. Since I woke up from my coma, I had only been back to Pat's a few times to pick up alcohol.

The room was medium sized and used every square inch of space. There was a main bar and a mini bar. A juke box to my left and a ping pong table to my right. A TV sat above the main bar and bar stools sat right by. There were several arcade games lined against the wall near the main door, and a large couch near the back, which I was now laying on.

Pat's Room was actually a small corner store that was just a block away from our apartment. I used to come here as a kid and always get candy. Pat wasn't as fat back then. The corner store, however, was only used as a front for his downstairs bar. You could enter from the back, which I always did, and go down a few steps into the store's basement. Then, Wah-la! You were now in the real Pat's Room. A small, illegally operated bar that he's apparently had since before I was even born.

"Started it with my bro and pops," he once told me. Both his father and brother were dead. I don't know how or why, and didn't feel it was my place nor business to ask.

I had my suspicions however, that it had to do with money and this illegal bar. On a few occasions I had seen Pat talking with some shady characters and seen him with a gun here and there.

But, like I told myself, it was none of my business. Besides, I never felt unsafe here at Pat's. I had known Pat since I could walk my way down here with a nickel in my pocket and ask for about twenty items. I found out about this place back in sophomore year of high school and have been coming here ever since.

Pat didn't mind. A paying customer was a paying customer. Although I had a bill that was ever growing since waking up from the coma. I told Pat that I would pay him soon. He let it go because I always paid off my debts with him.

He came out from the back room and made his way over to me. I watched him as the voice of Sinatra trickled over to me. I closed my eyes. "So kid?" he began, slapping my leg with a towel as he sat at the end of the couch. "How've you been?" I could smell his cigarette breath from here.

The question implied more than what was said. What Pat really wanted to know was: You tried to kill yourself and ended up killing someone else in the process. I can't believe it. Tell me more!

But I knew it was coming. I didn't know many people, but the ones that I did want to know:

Why did you do it?

How could you do it?

How do you feel about causing a woman's death?

They didn't outright ask me these questions, but they didn't have to. It was in their tone, their body language, and their sympathetic and accusing expressions. The tender touches to my shoulder. The "I'm here if you ever need me!" statements. The blatant staring when I walk outside my apartment.

I hated it. Hated it all.

Why couldn't I be invisible again? Dead to the world? I was never this popular in life as I felt after nearly dying.

Pat had avoided asking me about it, but there was no one else in the bar today so I guessed it seemed like a good time to bring it up.
I kept my eyes closed and inched my face forward in the direction of Pat's voice and gave a soft

"Hmm?"

Please Pat, let it go.

"So what's this I hear about you trying to kill yourself?"

Sigh.

I sat up and gulped down the last of my spritzer, sitting the empty can on the coffee table beside Pat's couch.

"What do you want to know, Pat?" I said, trying not to sound exasperated. I didn't want to seem upset that he was asking me, and I couldn't expect Pat to be any different than all the others. It *had* happened. It was real and I being here right now was living proof that I was not dead. But Melanie's absence was proof that she was gone and that there was no escaping the fact that it occurred.

No, I could not expect Pat to pretend to be blind and deaf to what was being said by others.

My jaw clenched tightly and my hands folded into fists as I lay there on Pat's couch. I hated it all. And everyone.

Nosy.

Judgmental.
Inconsiderate of my feelings.

They were all those things and more. But yet, I still couldn't blame them for being it all.

Who wouldn't want to know about the girl who tried to kill herself and survived, only to cause the death of her rescuer?

I opened my eyes and took a deep breath just as a shadow darted across the room and a familiar presence made my entire body tingle. The shadow ran up the side of the wall. My eyes drifted shut again. I didn't need to acknowledge the shadow to know what was happening.

It was Molly, and she was trying to get in, as she always did, when I was at Pat's. But for some reason Molly could never materialize here. I didn't know why. Was it because I was drunk? Already too real and honest with myself to deny anything?

Pat's Room was the one and only place Molly could not get into, and I loved it. Her torment of me was gone, at least here, for a few hours.

"Well?" Pat said, still waiting for an answer. I had almost forgotten he was still sitting nearby.

"What do you want to know?" I asked him again.

"C'mon, Jadey," he said, calling me by my obsolete childhood nickname. No one called me that anymore. I wouldn't respond to them even if they did. My name was Jayd. Like the gem. Get it right or fuck off.

I gave my silence.

"Jayd?" Pat asked again.

The room smelled like smoke, incense, and alcohol. I could hear people out and about outside the back door.

"Pat..." I began.

"Y' know Jayd, I knew someone who tried to kill herself. A girl I was close with. She died afterwards." His voice cut through me like a sharp blade.

I sat still and slowly opened my eyes. Pat sat at the end of the couch; an elbow propped up on the chair's arm. He wore a shirt two times too small and I could see every roll protruding behind his armpit-stained shirt. Sinatra continued to play in the background, but a different song this time.

Was he being serious? Pat often told me stories and many of them seemed so outrageous that I felt that they had to be complete bullshit. From being in a shootout with the police when he was a preteen, from nearly being abducted by what he believed were lizard people, to finding out an ex-girlfriend was an assassin. His stories were ridiculous and never failed to get a laugh out of me.

But something about Pat's tone made me go cold. I looked at him, looked at his bushy eyebrows that were turned downwards sullenly, looked at his eyes that were turned away, staring at the floor. I looked at his blotchy, sweaty face, that seemed to be in deep thought. That seemed so serious and ominous. So unlike Pat.

He had my attention now and I sat up a little, positioning myself to listen.

"She was a girl I used to like and we went to school together back home on the island. Her name was Daniella." Pat said. He faced me now as he spoke.

"She was pretty. Kinda like you. And smart as hell. She was popular and well-liked by everyone. Could have any guy she wanted. I had a big crush on her and she was nice to me, even though I knew she didn't like me like that."

I wonder if Melanie was popular in school? Loved by everyone?
"She liked to write," Pat continued. "Could write about anything. Short stories, long novels, articles, essays. All that shit. And poetry. She was good at poetry. We bonded over that. She would walk by my house and I would shout "Daniella! Tu escribes hoy?" and she would always say yes."

A writer? I wonder if Melanie was a writer? Was she the professional type of writer or did she do it as a hobby? Maybe she was working on her first novel when...

"Then one day we just got the call. We were all in the classroom and the principal came in and told us all that Daniella was dead. I didn't learn until later from my ma that she had hung herself in her closet and died a few days later after never regaining consciousness. Her parents had told the school that she was sick when she was really comatose the whole time."

Pat dug into his pocket and took out a box of cigarettes. He took out one, lit it and took a long draw before puffing the smoke into the air. As the smoke drifted over to me, I waved it away with a hand.

"We were all devastated. Me especially. Everyone wanted to know why?

Why did she do it? We never knew why." Pat said.

His answer floated in the smokey air as I laid back down and shut my eyes.

Why?

It was always the question after the fact.

I was starting to hate the word. Why?

Why this? Why that?

It was just a word. A tiny little word. But it was only that I had been, throughout my life, constantly asked why. Why are you crying, Jayd? Why are you so quiet, Jayd? Why do you look so upset today, Jayd?

Why, they would always ask. Never a *what* or a *when* or a *how*. Always a why.

I was beginning to despise it.

The word demanded an explanation that people didn't deserve. An explanation that the world didn't deserve.

It was only after the fact that people seemed to care. That they seemed to look. To listen. To feel. Did anyone ask Daniella how she was feeling that day? Or any day? Did they read between the lines of her dark stories or moody poetry? Did they look into her eyes and see the pain stirring behind them? The frown that was behind her smile? The cracking in her laugh? The cuts that were on her arms?

Maybe Daniella, despite being popular, felt invisible? Maybe she was really lonely? Maybe she was being abused? Maybe she was bipolar and was only putting on a facade?

We would never know why and maybe Daniella knew that those she left behind didn't deserve to.

"The poem she wrote and showed me before she died. I remember it till this very day," Pat said. "Before you leave, I want to give it to you."

He looked over at me and gave a small, sympathetic smile. He tapped my leg.

"Don't die on me kiddo." He said. "Who else will buy up all my liquor?"

A light chuckle escaped my lips. Pat always knew what to say to change the tone from serious to humorous. It was one thing I liked about him.

I stretched my arms and legs on the couch and sat up. Hours had passed and it was time to go home.

Swiftly getting up and putting on my sneakers, I gave Pat a quick pat on the shoulder and said see you later.
Before leaving, Pat called me back.

"Wait! Let me see if I can find it!" he yelled out. I took a few moments to realize that he was talking about the poem.

Pat ran upstairs to his apartment above the bar and store. I patiently waited.

Poetry used to be a drug to me. Hell, writing was once how I escaped the world for a few hours. Growing older, alcohol became my choice of an escape. Mama was sad that I stopped writing, and I felt a little guilt as well. But the pain had begun to be too much and writing...just didn't do it for me anymore. Poetry didn't protect older Jayd, whereas younger Jayd saw it as an immediate relief. The therapeutic sensation of jotting my emotions and thoughts on a page didn't allow me to escape reality anymore.

No one ever really read what I wrote anyway.

Minutes passed and after a while, thumps could be heard coming back down the stairs into the bar. Pat handed me a folded, crumbled, and water-stained piece of paper.

"You can keep it. I memorized it years ago" he told me.

"Thanks Pat," I replied as I turned and headed towards the exit.

Outside the sun shined brightly, and the air was humid. I took a moment for my eyes to adjust to the brightness.

Unfolding the piece of paper Pat gave me, I looked down to see if I could read what was written quickly, but stopped.

It was written entirely in Spanish.

Chapter 6

A black fluff ball sat on my chest as I nodded my head to the music pouring into my ears. I had the volume up high as I lay on my bed.

Sylvia let me go early today and said she would still pay me. She had really grown on me the past few weeks, but still remained stern and cordial with me. Sometimes I'd catch her quickly smiling at dry humor as she told me about growing up in Italy and moving here with her extended family.

Yellow-orange eyes looked over at me as I adjusted Norman's weight onto my stomach. He was getting fat. I stroked his face and back before settling back in my position and bobbing my head some more to the music.

It was Friday evening and the street below was filled with shouting, laughter, and people eagerly running about, looking for some fun and to get into trouble. Police sirens could be heard off in the distance. Yup. Normal people were out tonight enjoying themselves on a Friday evening.

Mama and Aunt Opal being one of them. I knew they were going out when I heard footsteps move down the hallway to my door. Mama popped her head in.

"Jayd, baby? Me and Opal going out. I left food on the table for you!" she said. She was all dolled up in red. Red lipstick, red eye shadow, and a bright red dress. Mama knew how to dress to impress, and her beauty only elevated her style.

Molly whistled suggestively as she glanced at Mama.
"Ok, Mama. See you later!" I watched her close the door then I laid back down, turning up the music louder. The beat pulsed against my eardrums

and little by little, I could feel the oncoming pain. I knew this wasn't healthy, but I wanted to drown out my thoughts with sound. I didn't want to think, because if I started thinking, I would start feeling. And if I started feeling I would start crying.

About what?

About...everything. That I didn't have any friends to do anything with tonight. That I didn't have any good memories to think about nor future events to look forward to. I looked down at my body.

It all felt so...hollow. So empty, despite the beat of my heart and the lifting of my cheat with each breath.

About never really fitting in or discovering my hobbies or aspirations. What goals did I have? Where was I heading? At this point, was I merely existing?

I couldn't even say I was a shell of my former self, because I was never fully whole to begin with.

A grumble erupted in the silence and my stomach tightened. I was hungry. Time to eat.

Shooting up from the bed and ignoring Norman's protests I ran out of my bedroom and towards the kitchen. Molly followed, sprinting after me. Why couldn't she just go away?

When I got to the kitchen I went straight to the table to see what Mama left. Sitting on the table was a plate, covered with a paper towel, and a piece of paper. I paused, then reached over to pick up the paper. After scanning it for a moment, I realized what it was. An application for a nearby local college. Mama must have left it here for me. I sat the paper down on the table.

As much as I loved her, I hated how pushy she could be sometimes. I had no intention of starting college this fall.

I sat down and dug into the beef stew and collard greens under the paper towel. I was about halfway through my dinner before I noticed a small white piece of paper sticking out from under my dinner plate. I was too busy stuffing my face to notice it at first.

Pulling it from under the plate, I peered at it. Scrawled on the paper was the name Janelle, and a phone number.

Janelle?

I pondered the name for a moment before I remembered what Mama had told me about the therapist that Dr. Corrandy had suggested. Mama must want me to give this lady a call.

A sigh escaped from my lips. Norman silently entered the room and sat at my feet under the table. Molly is sitting on the table, glancing at the college application.

The kitchen is quiet, except for the sounds that came from me. I could almost make out the voices of the couple next door. They were a new family that moved in, after Mrs. Diane retired from teaching and moved in with her daughter down in Virginia a year ago. I never personally met them. They didn't seem friendly.

"Crazy...sick...that girl.... feel sorry.... Mother..."

The words echoed in the silence of the kitchen. In my ears. In my head.

Were they talking about me?

Molly now had her ear to the wall, listening intently.

The drip of the kitchen faucet could now be heard. Mama must have forgotten to turn it off.

Molly was now swiftly back at the table with a wide grin on her face.

Yup. They're talking about you.

Of course, they are.

I tore into the beef stew and washed it down with some diet coke. With each mouthful, I barely chewed. Mama also told me to chew my food or I would choke.

When I was finished eating, I leaned back against the chair. Rumbles drifted to my ears and before I knew it I felt hungry again. Sluggishly walking over to the fridge to see if there was any more stew left, I was met with only an old half-eaten tuna sandwich, some juice, and a carton with a few drops of milk.
Time to order some pizza.
Running into my room and getting on my phone, I dialed and ordered a

large meat lovers pizza from the local pizzeria. One thing about living in New York was that there was always a place that had some bomb-ass pizza.

I sat back at the kitchen table, drifting in and out of my thoughts. It was quiet, and I didn't like it when it was quiet. The quietness forced me to observe the room. Forced me to reflect and think. And I didn't want to think. Because I would start to think about...her.

Her? Really Jayd. She has a name.

She *had* a name.

And the least you can do is acknowledge it.

I can't take this shit anymore. Before I knew it, my tears ducts were swelling, threatening to burst.

I wasn't planning on calling her today, or anytime soon really, but my fingers began to rapidly punch in the phone number, and in no time it began to ring.

"Hello?" a smooth voice said on the other line.

I didn't answer right away. I was too shocked that I had actually called her. What was I going to say anyway? I hadn't even thought of it. Just dialed.

"Hello?" The voice said again. "Is someone there?"

C'mon Jayd, don't be a creep.

"Hello..." I said into the phone, softly. Childlike.

"Hi! "Who is this?" the voice said.

"Uh...my name is Jayd. Jayd B-"

"Jayd?' the voice is exclaimed. "Oh yes, I heard about you! I was wondering when you'd come to see me!"

Really…? The voice that spoke to me sounded eager and excited, and also comforting.

"Oh Jayd, you caught me as I was just packing up to leave for the night. My office is closed in ten minutes."

"...I'm sorry" I said to Janelle. "I just wanted someone to talk to…"

"Of course, sweetheart! I'll stay on the phone for as long as you need me to." She sounded so endearing. I wondered what she looked like. From her tone, I get the feeling that she's seen and talked to many people like me and worse. Her words seemed to be carefully chosen and her pitch never got too loud or forceful. She was probably a very patient and perspective person growing up, or became that way later on.

"I... haven't been feeling well lately," I told her, stuttering.

Lately? When have you ever felt well? And why was I stuttering?

"I understand, and I'm glad that you called. Now tell me what's on your mind and describe how you're feeling to me. I care about and I am concerned about what you're feeling."

Of course, she does.

I glanced at the small, mahogany, clock that was nailed to the kitchen wall above the entrance. door.

"But it's late. Your office closes in ten minutes," I was hesitant. Why was I hesitant?

"That's Ok! I have the time!" she said.

Of course, she did.

"Well…" I began. "I've been struggling with...with...something that happened to me. Months ago." I took a breath as I prepared myself to say the next few words.

"I wasn't...feeling that well. On that day. On the bridge," I continued. "I was...on the bridge...and I...I…"

I trailed off, never finishing my contorted thoughts. I was digging at my brain now, unearthing that very day. But in my mind, it was raining hard. Flooding. And the more it rained the muddier my mind became and the more the hole that filled my memory of that day became unreachable.

I could hear Janelle softly breathing on the other end. She was being patient with me, and I appreciated it. But it was fruitless. I wasn't going to talk tonight.

After a few seconds of silence, she spoke.

"It's alright Jayd," she said. "Sometimes we form blockages as a means to protect ourselves from traumatic past events. You don't have to tell me anything you aren't comfortable with and you're free to share what you want when you're ready. We'll go at your own pace."

I breathed in deeply, both to calm myself and as a display of relief. At this moment, talking to her, I knew I would love Janelle.

"I'm free this Sunday morning," she told me. "Just for you. You can come into my office or we can meet somewhere else. Whatever you're comfortable with, Jayd."

"Ok." was all I replied.

"We'll take it slow," Janelle concluded. "I want to help you, Jayd. In any way, I can. Let's get together on Sunday. I'll phone your mother tomorrow and let her know. I'll see you Sunday! Goodnight, sweetheart!"

"Goodnight..." I said, and hung up. I noticed that she waited for me to hang up first.

Norman is still under the table, silently caressing my leg. I bent down to stroke him.

I thought about Melanie. I wonder if she had a cat? Or any pets at all. Do they miss her? How were they doing now?

I felt my eyes begin to swell and the feeling of guilt washed over me again.

Janelle.

I think I'm going to like you, Janelle.

The tears start to fall. I let them stream down my face, not bothering to wipe them away.

Molly watched me, silently, in the corner.

Chapter 7

The first thing I like to do when I walk into a therapist office is to gaze around and take in everything. From their walls to their tables, their cabinets to their windows, and from their desk to the chair that I'll be sitting in and the one that they'll be. I look at the items on their desk to discover who they are and what they're about. Sometimes therapists would be like what I would call: The Basics. Standard white or benign walls with stock photos hanging on them. Traditional wooden furniture and the typical family photos on their desk. Behind them was a plaque and certificate, their pride and joy. A message to all who entered to understand that they were professionals, qualified and great at what they do because they studied and were given a piece of paper that told them so. They were dull and boring, and they were the ones that were mocked in the media as coining the phrase "So how does that make you feel?" as their patient lay on a couch and they wrote on their clipboard.

Then there were: The Wackos. The funky, jolly, eccentric therapists who believed in aliens, thought marijuana was a godsend and was exactly what their patients should use to ease their depression. They always had upbeat music playing in the background as they studied and diagnosed you.

Another group was what I would call: The Libbies. They were the young, liberal, avocado toast eating, coffee binge drinking, gentrifying yet open-minded, arthouse, down with the struggle, LGBTQ friendly therapists. They annoyed me to no end, and I actively avoided them. Most tried to equate my anxiety to my race or gender, but it was more than that. I never felt more misunderstood when I was in their presence. I liked many of the things they stood for, but it was like they were wearing a mask and putting on a play when they spoke about the world's struggles. They seemed phony, and the type that could always go back to their safe space when shit got tough, whereas the rest of us were stuck.

I had long divided up the groups of therapists I had encountered over my life while being their patient.

However, with Janelle, as she sat beside me on her couch, I knew she did not fall into any of those groups. She was in her own lane. And she was direct, while also offering warmth and true understanding.

I leaned into the couch with my knees up, facing her. As she sat opposite me and I examined her entirely.

She was gorgeous, with clear brown skin, large doe-like watery brown eyes, full lips, a button nose, and her kinky hair pulled back into a bun. She wore casual clothing in the form of jeans and a T-shirt with some sandals.

If I could imagine her as a mythical creature, she would be some woodland nymph.

"You're very sensitive. I can see it in your eyes. Very attentive and alert. Have you always been like that, Jayd?

I sat up straight and my attention veered back to listening to her, as the question had caught me by surprise. Usually, I was the one observing others intently.

"I... I'm not sure." I told her. "I guess so"

"Hmmmmm," was all she replied.
The window behind her desk was opened wide and the wind, as well as the birds, fluttered in. One cute bird, in particular, landed on her desk, looked at us, turned around and flew back out of the window. I eyed her

desk. It had small crystals lined on each end and I recognized a few of the crystals. There were also some small framed paintings and drawings surrounding the corners of the desk and going into a circle. The pieces of art ranged from stick figures to what looked like art that was done by a professional. I wonder if her other clients had painted those? That's nice of her to frame them on her desk. I used to paint a lot when I was younger. I liked writing more though. Poetry is the best.

I wonder if Melanie liked to paint or write? Was she any good at it? Did Melanie have any special hobbies?

"Jayd" came the silky, honey-drenched voice of Janelle. "Jayd, sweetheart, I need you to get out of your head for a moment. Try to push past those constant thoughts; those interruptions that come in, and get out of your head."

Molly was behind Janelle now, leaning forward with her leg on the couch arm. I had noticed her earlier when she came with me this morning to visit Janelle, but as usual, I tried my best to ignore her. But she was heavily making her presence known to me as she angled herself above Janelle. She was frowning. I looked down at my hands, then back up at Janelle.

"What keeps you in your head, Jayd?" Janelle asked me, moving gently towards me.

I hesitated before responding, making sure I was replying with the truth. At least the half-truth.
"I like it there". I told her. "It helps when I'm imaging. It keeps me distracted"
"Imaging?" Janelle replied. "What is imaging, Jayd?"

Was I going to tell her? Let her into my world of over-analyzing, over-stressing, and worst of all, over-feeling?

"No," I mistakenly said out loud before I could catch myself.

"No what, Jayd?"

Damn, I thought. I did it again. Jayd, why are you such a fucking weirdo? Why couldn't I keep my thoughts in my head and never let them spill out from my mouth?

No, I decided.

I wasn't ready to tell Janelle about my inner world of imaging. Because she would ask me why I do it, and then I would have to explain that my mind has been on auto-pilot for most of my life.

And especially now.

Especially now because of what happened with Melanie.

I didn't respond to Janelle, clouded in my thoughts on imaging, so I was a bit startled when I heard her speak up.

"I want to help you Jayd, but I'm not going to coddle you." she said, once again moving intently towards me again. "I would like to get to the root of your anxiety, and I would like you to acknowledge what's underneath it all as well."

She was sincere, and I knew it. I could hear it in her voice and see it in her body language. The framed portraits that lined her desk said that she was not only endeared by her patients' artwork, but proud of them.

She wore no mask. Not like all the other therapists who I knew only cared because they were getting paid, or because they got off on feeling superior, perhaps god-like in their assistance of aiding the mentally ill. They were there only for their own benefit, but they would never admit it. I knew those therapists well. I knew people like that in general. They are your teachers. Your doctors. Many times, even your friends and your family.

I wasn't a broken glass that needed to be mended, I wasn't a dying flower than needed to come alive again, and I wasn't some fucking piece that didn't fit into the puzzle.

She said she wasn't going to coddle me, and I didn't want to be coddled. I didn't want anyone's sympathy. I wanted people to understand. Simple fucking understanding.

"Jayd, I know about what happened to you on that bridge. And just before you ask, no, none of your family members told me. I read about you. I like to gather as much information on my patients before I see them. But like I told you earlier, we won't talk about it until you're comfortable enough."

I sat in silence, not really listening to her, but neither tuning her out. I suppose I was meant to be shocked by this information, yet I felt nothing. I just sat there and thought many thoughts.

Did everyone know about me and what I did? Of course they did, it was front page news at the time.

Why couldn't I ever be accepted the way I was? Maybe it wouldn't be so bad then to feel everything all of the time.

I wonder if I'm still in a coma, and this is all just one massive, horrible, nightmare. But of course, it wasn't, because that meant that I could wake up from it all. And life wasn't that fair.

"Jayd?" Janelle said, pulling me from my thoughts again. "Please listen to me Jayd."

"I'm sorry," I said quietly.

"Jayd, I need you to pull away from that enclosure in your head. I need you to come out of there and talk to me. Could you do that for me? We can't get through this together unless you make the effort."

I looked into her eyes. My eyes felt watery and I knew I would have tears streaming down my face soon. She was asking too much of me now. It was too early; too soon. Maybe it always will be. I wasn't willing to part from the only place I could completely be me.

"Jayd…" she began again. She wanted a definite answer.

"Ok...no...no I can't," I said, defensively. "But it's ok...I have a plan."

"A plan," Janelle looked at me in confusion.

"Janelle," I said, calling her by her first name as she had given me permission to on introduction. "What do you see when you look at me? And please tell me the truth."

Her eyes widened and she stared into my face. For a few seconds she studied me. When she spoke it was like tasting honey.

"I see a beautiful and intuitive girl who's been through a traumatic event. I see a girl who doesn't give herself enough credit and who needs more self-love and a positive self-esteem for who she is."

I took in her words silently, but slowly nodded, letting her know that I heard her.

"Jayd," she continued. "I want you to learn to be kinder to yourself. I can see that you're battling with yourself inside, but is unwilling to let herself heal. I want you to be better to yourself."

Molly mocked Janelle as she spoke with exaggerated movements. I seriously wished she would disappear forever.

"I know it's our first-time meeting, but I would like for you to do something for me."

I was looking at her again. She looked into my eyes. Tears were going to fall any second.
"Jayd, I want you to start writing down positive affirmations and compliments about yourself. Write down a list, nothing long, maybe five things that you love about yourself, or even just mildly like."
"Write down positive affirmations that you believe, or would like to believe, will come true. Do this every day, and when you come in next time, I want you to read them out to me."
She paused. "And I hope you then can tell me about this plan of yours."
I nodded again.

Chapter 8

I watched her mouth open and close, words flying out but I heard nothing. I consistently blocked her out when she talked to me and had become quite good at it over time. She raged on and on, her lips flapping in the wind, but she might as well have been yelling nothing at all.

Why can't you just go away? Leave forever?

I wanted to ask her this, but knew better. Mama was right behind her and would immediately scold me in disbelief for my rudeness towards my aunt.

Aunt Opal and I were arguing about my first paycheck I received from Sylvia's. I stood in my bedroom doorway as both my mom and my aunt stood in the hallway. It was dark in the hallway because Mama had turned off the lights. Lights made the summer heat unbearable.

"It's my money, Aunt Opal," I said quietly.

"And is this your house, girl?" she bellowed back.

Mama inched forward gently and purposefully. She could sense the escalation in the argument getting worse. The smell of fried fish lingered in the air around us. Mama was cooking baked mac and cheese and hushpuppies along with the fish. The aroma made my stomach growl, but my irritation with Aunt Opal was beginning to overcome my hunger.

"It's all of ours, Aunt Opal," I replied back calmly.

Aunt Opal huffed.
"I don't see you paying any bills around here little girl!" she shot back.

"The little money you do earn needs to go towards the household! I'm sick of your sass mouth! And let's not forget how much you cost us all in medical bills cause you…

"Opal!" Mama stopped her just in time before she could finish her sentence.

It didn't matter anyway. I knew what she meant before the realization hit us all. We owed the hospital thousands of dollars due to my stay after my...accident...on the bridge. After I tried to kill myself. After I caused Melanie to die.

It had dawned on me, although it was something that I tried to block out, that Mama had picked up a part-time job in addition to the full-time one she had so that she could put that extra money towards my hospital bills. Mama worked more now than she ever did, with the days of her being just a homemaker gone. I knew, and of course felt guilty, every time I saw her get up on the weekends and leave again after she came home from work on the weekdays. I saw the tiredness behind the strength and beauty of her hazel-colored eyes, and I saw the exhaustion behind the weak smiles she gave me.

Truthfully, I had no real purpose in spending my money on anything other than alcohol and snacks. The money would be better spent on household bills. Or my hospital bills.

But still, it was money I earned and money that brought me things that I enjoyed. And I definitely didn't want Aunt Opal telling me what to do with it.

Behind my mother I could see Molly floating in the back, her head cocked amusingly at the scene, hoping for a climax from me. She wouldn't be getting one.

My eyes stabbed holes through my aunt as I glared at her, and then they drifted behind her to look at my mother. Those tired eyes looked at me with a mixture of love and... fear?

Why was Mama afraid? Did she think Aunt Opal's words would cause me to…?

No. I shouldn't even think of it.

"I'm sorry, Mama", I spoke to her as I ignored my aunt standing in front of me. "You can have the money I get."

"Jayd…" Mama started. Aunt Opal glared at me

"No, it's fine." I cut her off. "I wasn't really going to do anything much with it anyway."

Aunt Opal huffed. Her arms were crossed as she shifted her body to one side from the other. I could see Mama clearly now. She was so beautiful, even when she looked exhausted.

I studied her face, as I had done thousands of times before, and it brought me back to a place that I didn't want to go.

A place where little me was at the supermarket with Mama. It was a few days before the Thanksgiving holiday and Mama was doing some last minute shopping for a peach cobbler. I had happily skipped along with her, wanting to get out of the house and see all the fall decorations around. I loved the fall. The colors of the leaves, the smells of cinnamon and pumpkin, and the warm and cozy feeling. School was out for the holiday, and there were many parents and children alike at the market.

I wore a white shirt, a knee-length jean skirt, white sneakers, and a jacket. Mama wore one of her long-sleeved, floor length dresses with a light shawl around her shoulders. Her hair and makeup were done up to beautifully match the fall season. I loved going out with her when I was younger as she would get so many stares and compliments from strangers. I felt proud to have such a beautiful mother and to stand in her presence.

Until after that day in the supermarket before Thanksgiving.

Mama spotted a woman, one of her old high school friends and they quickly began chatting and catching up. I held her hand as she led me over. The friend had a boy with her, around my age. She introduced him as her son and Mama introduced me as her daughter.

Mama's friend sized me up and I knew by the way she looked at me, she was slightly disappointed. She gave a fake smile and in a sickly inauthentic voice said:

"My! Don't you look just like your Mama!"

Her son peered at me and his eyes widened.

I braced myself as I could feel the overwhelming emotion pour out before a word even left his mouth

"No she doesn't! She's not as pretty!" the boy said loudly. "Look at her!"

Instinctively, I gripped Mama's hand that I held.

The store was packed and there were many people in earshot. It grew quiet as people around glanced at us. Mama was silent, as was her friend. I could feel both of their eyes on me, but I was staring straight ahead, down the aisle of canned goods. Eyes from strangers burned into my back and sides. Shocked gasps, snickers, and whistles rattled around me, but I dare not look at the faces who were making the noises.

I gripped Mama's hand tighter.

I was looking at all of the canned food. Red cans, blue cans, yellow cans. All filled with yummy food. What didn't we go over and pick some up? I bet they all tasted good. Why were we just standing here? What did we come here to get again? Oh, that's right! We needed to get the pastry dough. Well, this wasn't the right aisle! Silly Mama! We needed to go... go somewhere.

Somewhere else...

"Jayd..." a distorted voice said.

I felt a warm, familiar presence near me and felt a hand softly touch my shoulder. I knew it was Mama but I was too far away, down the aisle.

No Mama! This wasn't the right aisle! This wasn't the right place! Grab my hand and let's go! Go away. Go somewhere else. Anywhere else. Where the strangers weren't staring at me and where we could find the dough. Not here.

"Jayd!" The voice was louder this time. My grip on her hand was ironclad.

I didn't want her to get away. I didn't want her to ever leave. I needed to be in Mama's presence. Her sunshine and ocean breeze presence. Like the silver cans that sat next to the colored ones, I was the silver and Mama was the colored. Like an old black and white movie next to the colored remake, I was the old and Mama was the new. The colorful, the lively, the charismatic, the beautiful. She was the pretty version to my dull, lifeless, gray aura. My lines weren't as finely drawn as hers. My voice is not as dreamy. My presence wasn't as memorable. I made people uncomfortable when I was around them. Mama could soothe even Satan's damned soul.

I was gripping her hand so tight it must be hurting her terribly by now. Pinching into her skin.

That fine, smooth, delicate skin Mama had.

But I had too.

She couldn't step away. Not for a moment. If she did, I would be standing here all alone. And that would be worse than dying. What would I be if not the shadow of my mother?

But why were we still standing here? We needed to go find the dough! The strangers' voices were louder now and they were buzzing all around me like bees. They were sharp echoes that pieces my skull. Was someone...laughing?

"Jayd!!" The voice pierced through all the others like a blade. I felt water on my neck, rolling down slowly. And I was floating in the air now, lifting off the ground. An angry sharp voice pierced through the strangers' voices again. Mama's friend and her son then came into view. They were watching me.

Mama's friend looked so apologetic and the boy was red faced as his mother gripped his shirt and scolded him.

A soft, warm kiss pressed against my cheek. I could smell Mama's perfume and knew that I was in her embrace.

In reality I had been silently crying and staring, in a daze, down the canned goods aisle. Mama had picked me up and marched away as she threw insults back at her friend over keeping her rude ass little brat's mouth shut.

All the while I still gripped Mama's hand tightly. She was nice enough to not tell me to let go. We were going away now, somewhere else. Maybe we were going to get the dough. Or maybe we were going home. I don't really remember much after that. I just remember the overwhelming feeling I had felt of relief that we were moving away from all the noise.

I didn't go out with Mama that much anymore. And when I did, I made sure that my headphones were in and I could block out all of the noise and voices.

The muffled voices of conversation were going on outside of my head and I could make out Mama and Aunt Opal's voices, but not what they were saying.

Had I been standing here, daydreaming for long?

Time to wake up.

I snapped out of my thoughts and focused my attention back on Mama.

Her eyebrows were arched up in deep concern. Aunt Opal's ghastly voice spoke up.

"Little girl, were you even listening?" she demanded. I was silent. Mama spoke up then.

"Jayd honey...I don't want your money. But we need more of it coming into this house." She moved towards me until she stood directly in front of me. The dim light in my room illuminated her face. I could smell her perfume. It was another luxury brand this time.

"Time's are hard right now baby" she went on. "I just got another bill from the hospital. We can't afford this one without seriously cutting back."

"And *we* ain't going to be cuttin' back because *we* didn't rack up that bill!" Aunt Opal remarked.

"Opal, please!" Mama wailed, angrily. She turned around and glared at her sister. They stood staring each other down before Aunt Opal's face softened in defeat. Even Aunt Opal was no match for Mama.

I watched as Aunt Opal thankfully turned around and walked off. Mama turned back to me.

"Jayd, baby, I know you're not well," she said gently.

"But please...consider helping out a bit whenever you can. I tried to get them to lower the bill, and they did the first time. We don't qualify for assistance. I need you to reach out to the hospital and plead with them. If not for a lesser bill, then at least for a due date extension."

I nodded, letting Mama know I understood.

She leaned forward and kissed my forehead.

"Now, time to go to work." She handed me a paper bag that I hadn't even noticed she had in her hand. It was lunch.

As she walked away, I watched her; wishing that I could just merge my body into her's, becoming her. In a perfect world I would be her identical twin in mannerisms and looks.

Without wasting much time, I grabbed my jacket and my bag, kissed Norman who was soundly asleep on my bed, and headed out the door, down the hallway stairs, and out of the apartment.

Flashes of cars and people went by as I ran down the blocks, making my way to Sylvia's. In about fifteen minutes, I was standing outside of my workplace. I ran inside, put down my things, and ran to the back to get on my apron and gloves. Sylvia was at the register and had nodded over at me as a way of saying, "Hi, you're here. Now get to work."

I was getting good at my job and Sylvia would occasionally allow me to place orders and answer calls for her in addition to my usual work. Although far from friends, Sylvia and I respected each other and grew to like one another.

I found out she had only one son who had found a woman to marry back in Italy, where he lived full time. Sylvia would bemoan spending the days without her four grandchildren, and she greatly looked forward to the upcoming holidays when her son and his family would visit. Sylvia's husband was long dead. He smoked a lot throughout his life and developed lung cancer. He was gone in a few months after the diagnosis.

I began cleaning the shelves and organizing antiques that recent customers had moved out of place. When I had finished, I was ready to restock some of the lower shelves with new, smaller antiques that we had in the back. Before I did this, I went up to Sylvia.

"Yes?" she said as she glanced over at me, her glasses sitting on her nose and her tiny frame propped up on her stool. She was eating a bagel and drinking coffee.

"Sylvia...would it be alright if I could work overtime?" I stammered a little. "You know...to earn a little more?"

She stared silently at me, her face showing no emotion. She peered at me and looked me over. She didn't answer right away and for a few moments I wondered if I should have even asked.
Finally, she responded.

"Sure. Do what you like. Hourly rate is still the same, though. No time and a half. No extra." She turned back to her coffee and bagel.

I breathed a sigh of relief as I turned around and headed to the back of the store to the storage closet. I brushed past Molly, who was bending over and examining an antique of a little music box with a ballerina inside. She tried winding it up, but of course, she could not. She looked frustrated. I chuckled.

Chapter 9

The sweet aroma of allspice and peaches filled the air. The smell filled out every inch of the tiny kitchen. The windows were closed, as were the doors. The smells were strong and suffocating, and I loved it. Mama and I were making peach cobbler, and I was kneading the dough as she made the filling. Aunt Opal was in her room with the door shut, watching TV.

Baking was one thing Mama and I enjoyed doing together. Otherwise, we were very different and although we loved each other very much, I knew that we simply didn't get each other. But baking, and eating, was one thing we liked to do together. Younger me was always excited to bake with Mama. Young Jayd would be hopping up and down like a little bunny, yapping away as Mama gathered all of the ingredients. She, of course, would be the main one putting everything together, as no one could compete with Mama's cooking. But she enjoyed her little assistant from time to time and I always loved licking the utensils after she was done using them.

I still had that little spark in me that lit up when we would bake together, although it was much more muted. I was older and much more hardened. Baking with Mama brought out the younger, innocent Jayd out of me, and I enjoyed her presence like I enjoyed Mama's.

Moving my hands in a circular motion, I kneaded the dough and flattened it with a roller. On low volume, Nat King Cole played in the background.

"Baby, hand me the sugar," Mama asked me. I reached for the large glass jar of sugar we had sitting under the cabinets near the kitchen sink. Once handed over, I watch her measure out a cup. She was humming along to the music while rhythmically tapping her foot. I turned back to kneading the dough.

These were the moments in life that I wish would stay on repeat forever.

But, like every good moment in my life, it came to an abrupt end.

Loud, harsh, laughter erupted from above us, followed by a series of swearing and the sound of furniture being knocked over. A sudden scream then followed.

In the corner of my eye I could see Mama paused mid stir, and stand as still as a statue. I didn't bother even looking up though. I knew who it was making the commotion and I honestly wished they had moved out years ago.

A deep sigh escaped from Mama's lips accompanied by the roll of her eyes as she continued stirring.

The Palmers were drunkenly fighting again, as they had done for the past ten years. No amount of calling the police or trying to intervene on our parts mattered. Mrs. Palmer would always go back to Mr. Palmer and rebuff our aid. The last time Mama spoke to Mrs. Palmer, the woman had told Mama to mind her own business and get her own man, then maybe Mama wouldn't be so nosy and always in their business.

Mama never spoke to Mrs. Palmer again after that, nor tried to intervene. Aunt Opal never cared to begin with, and I was always in my head, trying to drown out all of the noise they made.

Mrs. Palmer probably grew up surrounded by abuse. It's normal to her. She probably doesn't even know what a healthy relationship is. She's scared to lose him, and would rather accept trash than to have no man at all.

Mama suddenly turned to me and cocked her head. It took me a moment to realize that I had just spoken out loud and hadn't kept my commentary in my head. I glanced at Mama.

She paused and looked me in the eyes. Then a small smile spread across Mama's perfectly shaped lips as she went back to mixing. "There you go, doing it again!" she bemused.

"Doing what?" I asked in confusion, still looking at her. It was a silly question because I knew exactly what she was talking about.

"That thing you always do, Jayd. Imaging." Mama answered, as she put her mixing spoon down and walked over to the stove to turn on preheating.

Oh, but of course.

Imaging. The thing that I always did when I focused on something or someone. I'd zoom in and analyze and hypothesize about it or the situation, trying to make sense of it, and coming to a conclusion of explaining it away. It scared me ever since Mama gave it a name. It came naturally like second nature to me, and I never thought to give it a name. She almost made it sound like a condition.

Mama said it started when I was toddler, and would point out and comment on things far beyond needing to. Or I would describe something and analyze why it was like that, why people were like the way they were, and acted and looked the way they were. Why society and life was the way it was. Aunt Opal called it nosiness and rudeness, Mama called it Imaging, because like an image, I would capture a scene and imagine all kinds of scenarios and reasons for why that image was the way it was.

If the question "What's the meaning of life?" was a person, Mama said it would be me.

"Is it so bad?" I asked, turning back to the dough. At this point, it was as flat as the cutting board and it was time to go into the pan. I reach for a stick of butter that I had taken out of the refrigerator earlier. It had softened nicely and I began buttering the pan in which the peach cobbler would go in. "What's wrong with noticing things?"

Mama chuckled. "Nothing, Jayd," she said. "But you don't just notice things. Never have."

"You analyze everything and always have a plausible story to go with it," she continued. "I said it many times before, you're a very observant and emotional girl."

I continued listening to her as I finished buttering the pan and began to spread out the dough.

"Even when the situation didn't concern you, you always knew what was going on and explained why. Could never watch the news around you when you were younger."

It was sad, but true. Younger Jayd and even now, hated listening and watching the news. It brought out so many emotions all at once. Many that I didn't want to feel.

"I would switch the channel every time I was watching it when you would come in," Mama said. "You cried and got upset about anything and everything happening around the world. Even bad weather."

I felt my throat tighten and a mild pain in my head. Aunt Opal would deliberately turn to the news in the morning when I got up and Mama wasn't around. I could sense the smugness off of her as the news anchors voices bellowed from out of her room. I would, of course, abruptly turn around, curse her, and head back to my room or the living room where the family TV was. The kitchen was my second favorite place in the apartment, and unfortunately Aunt Opal's room was right next to it.

"There was one time, and I'll never forget it," Mama continued. "When you came running into the living room and the TV was off. I was sitting there and you came running in and asking me to turn on the TV."

I paused from filling out the pan with dough and turned to her. I didn't remember the memory she was talking about now but it intrigued me.

"You told me to turn on the TV to the news," Mama said. "You were all upset and everything, telling me that someone killed them. I didn't know what you were talking about but I turned to the news to see what you were getting all upset about there was a story about a murder-suicide of an entire family by the husband."

Mama was looking at me now and I at her. We stood there at the kitchen counter staring each other in the eyes. The room had gone quiet now, even with the music playing and the sound of our neighbors above and kids playing below. The noise had all but drowned out.

"Jayd, the next thing you said gave me the chills" Mama's voice was low. "You told me: "You see Mama, they're dead. He killed them. I knew it! Mama, I knew it!"

"And then you ran back into the room and went back to sleep. Sound asleep."

We stood staring before Mama broke eye contact and went back to mixing. I turned back to the dough. I didn't know what to say, or if I should say anything at all. I didn't remember what she was talking about. Not at all. It was like I was hearing her talk about someone else. I felt...shame... from the girl in her story. What a weirdo. I would never creep Mama out like that. And to just go back to sleep...like nothing? That couldn't have been me. How would I have even known what was going on in the news? Mama must be mistaken.

But I knew she wasn't. Mama never lied to me and had no reason to.

I finished spreading the dough throughout the pain and pushed it over to Mama. I needed to leave now. This was one of those rare times when I didn't want to be in Mama's presence.

"I'm going for a walk," I told her. "I'll be back before dinner."

Before Mama could object, I gave her a quick kiss and then I was out the kitchen, out the front door, and down the apartment main stairs.

Feeling it before seeing it, I stopped when I felt gossip in the air. It was a strange mix of callousness and excitement in their tones as I grew closer to the main exit door. Whoever they were, they were talking loudly and were sitting on the front stoop to our apartment. I could only hear mumbles, so I decided to inch closer and put my ear to the door. I could just make out what they were saying.

"Lord Gina, I feel so bad for that lady!" came the first voice. "Her aunty has been telling me what her sister has got to put up with that girl. I don't know why they just don't put her in a mental asylum!"

"Girl, I know!" came the second voice. "I couldn't deal with it! She would have to go! The way Opal says she's been acting and talking, sounds like she has lost her mind! That girl always did look strange to me even when she was little. I feel for the mother."

"That mama ain't never gonna get a man with a daughter like her around," the second voice spoke again. "That would turn a man off a mile away! Girl trying to kill herself! Hhmp! I don't know what the hell is wrong with children these days! They're demented!"

I swung open the door and shuffled out. Ignoring the startled gasps of surprise and embarrassment, I walked down the front stairs and out into the street. The smell of cheap perfume and cigarettes trailed me as I kept it moving. I didn't even want to turn around and see who they were. They were all the same to me. Faceless, irrelevant, strangers in the world of many.

Cars honked their horns as they sped past and people walked on the sidewalks heading in all directions. It was warm today, but more of a milder warm day. Fall was around the corner.

I tried to keep my mind on my destination. I didn't want to think about what those women were talking about or what Mama had told me. A mental block was beginning to form already and I could feel it. Hidden in the back of my mind is what I believe were the memories I didn't want to remember. Earlier today was one of those memories. Peach cobbler be damned.

I seamlessly maneuvered my way around the crowds and across the streets, heading for the bus stop.

I hopped on the bus when it arrived and was nearing my destination rapidly. Taking deep breaths in and out, I told myself that I was finally ready for this.

What are you doing? Where are you going?

Molly had appeared and was sprinting beside me, but I, as usual, ignored her.

When I emerged through the door of her office, I didn't give her time to speak or get up. I wanted her to just listen. A look of surprise shrouded her face when she saw me. She had been typing on her laptop and a mound of books were stacked around her.

"Oh...Jayd? Hello!" she said.

"Janelle, I'm ready to talk about Melanie," I eagerly told her. "And about my plan."

Chapter 10

Hopefulness and hopelessness drifted all around. Both gloomy and cheery chatter of the staff and cries and laughs of the patients and their loved ones. The sterile, clean scent mixed with the funk of unwashed bodies and sickness clogged my nose. The direct and stern doctors gave their orders, and the nurses sucked their teeth. Exhaustion and annoyance. Eagerness and excitement. The halls flooded with people from all walks of life. Women in labor, the elderly, the young, the drug addicted, the accident victims and the generally sick and desperate. People looked at you, but not really. They had more important business here. The smell of death and despair and relief was too much for me.

I hate hospitals.

Was it the memories that they brought back? Or the overwhelming emotions and energy that I felt from each and every person? I couldn't decide.

With my jacket zipped up to my chin and my bag hanging across my torso, I stood in front of the nurses' desk, waiting for a nurse to finish talking on the phone, or the other one beside her to look up from her computer.

I had gone over what I would be saying in my head thousands of times. After all, I was here to plead, and I had to be as convincing as possible for them to lower or extend the payment for my medical bills.

I decided to sound as sincere and honest as possible, but not to let on that we're desperate.

The worst they could do was say no.

"Ahem," I said, clearing my throat and attempting to have the nurses acknowledge that I've been standing at their desk for the past ten minutes.

Neither looked up nor made any inclination that they had heard me. I tried again.

"Umm, excuse me?" I said softly.

The nurse on the computer slowly turned her head to me, yet kept her eyes on her screen.

"Yes?" was all she said.

I hesitated before answering and in an instant, I realized that I had over-analyzed in my head on what I would say but not how I would start it off.

After not answering right away the nurse peeled her eyes from her screen and glanced at me.

"Can I help you?" she said in slight irritation.

"Umm...yes," I began hesitantly. I was suddenly beginning to get light-headed. I didn't know if it was from all of the sounds and smells, or my own anxiety. I wanted to be locked in my room right now.

"Uh, yes, hi," I began again, this time injecting some confidence into my tone. "I was a patient here months ago and I need to discuss with some-one here about possibly lowering the bills we received or giving us an extension on the deadline. You see, we can't afford to take out anymore loans and my family and I..."

"We don't lower bills. If you'd like to discuss it with the doctor that assisted you, you'll have to make an appointment. Extensions are only given in emergencies and extreme cases. We're busy right now, thank you."

Her words cut into me like a knife. It wasn't that she interrupted me or that I had to relay the bad news to Mama, it was her general callousness and snootiness.

A body pressed against my side, and then moved between the space that I stood and the nurses desk. It was Molly.

She propped her elbow on the nurse's desk and cupped her chin, smirking at me. I watched her as she motioned towards a cup of coffee sitting beside the nurse that was still on the phone. She pointed to me and made a movement as if picking up the cup and then emptying its contents out on top of the head of the rude nurse I had just spoken to.

I turned away from Molly and locked eyes on the floor. Then, I looked back up at the nurse, before looking down again.

She was enormous. Not just her size and height, but her presence as well. Before even talking with her, I knew she might be either the head nurse or manager here. She had badly dyed blonde hair and her black roots were showing. The wrinkles and dark circles on her face reminded me of Mama's when she would come home from working late, except Mama still managed to look elegant and pretty despite being tired. Her hands were pudgy and I didn't see a wedding ring on her finger. Her nails were polished a lovely shade of blue, though. She felt like the bossy type. The bully type. I bet most nurses take commands from her, yet despise her and mock her behind her back. I wonder if she knew that?

Maybe she liked the power that it gave her, and didn't care? Maybe she was lonely, tired, and had worked all her life and was miserable? Maybe she didn't think it had been worth it?

Or was she sick of answering questions all day? Too much work on her plate? Maybe she was just as sick of the noise and smells as I was?

Or maybe she was just a miserable, bitter, bitch who took any chance she got to exert a god-like complex?

"Did you hear me?" an annoyed voice asked. My head shot up from the floor and I looked back at the desk. It was the nurse again, and this time she was glaring at me.

I didn't answer her. Instead, I looked straight at her. My eyes roamed every tip of her face. From her long nose to her deep-set eyes. Her lips were plump and curved. Her skin was the color of cashews. She must have been prettier when she was younger, but most of that beauty had faded away.

Molly snickered, and then proceeded to exaggerate movements with her stomach and arms, mocking the nurse's size.

"Whatever," I said abruptly before turning around only to stop dead in my tracks.

He was far away enough that he couldn't spot me, and his head was turned downward, talking to a nurse. The biggest hole opened up in my stomach and I could feel my legs getting lighter. My heart pounded against my chest. Was that him? Was it really him?

I knew him. I never forgot a face. Even though he was turned to the side, I knew it was him. Tall, broad shoulders. And his hair...

I clenched my bag to my side tightly. The noises seemed to drown out as I focused on the man standing far off in front of me, many feet away. The echoes of everything around me bounced off the walls and hit my eardrums. I could no longer smell this place and it was getting hazy.

But how...why was he here?

And like as if to answer my question, fate lifted the man's eyes from the nurse and looked directly my way. Our eyes met in an instance.

I bolted the opposite way towards the exit like lighting, not pausing to say excuse me or watch who or what was around me. Colors of people and the world flashed by as I ran down the hall, down a flight of stairs, and out of an exit. My lungs were crying in pain and my heart pounded so loud I felt that it would soon burst. My feet had a mind of their own and kept on running and running. Running to a familiar place.

Out of the hospital, across the street, down the blocks and towards that familiar place.

I don't know how long I ran, nor how fast. I didn't waste a second thinking about it.

When I burst through the basement door of Pat's place, I pushed past people and into the back room. I didn't see Pat nor was I looking for him. Some people were playing pool as I zoomed past them into the bathroom in the back. Bursting through the door, I shut and locked it quickly.

And then I collapsed on the floor.

Chapter 11

"Oh Jayd, I think that's a wonderful idea!"

This was the response Janelle had given me when I told her what I was planning on doing soon.

We were once again on her couch. This time I was laying down as I talked to her. The couch was a large cushion couch that expanded the entire wall. It was incredibly soft, yet firm in the right places. I almost felt like drifting off to sleep from the comfort before Janelle's response.

"And I think that's the right step for the acceptance and closure that you need," Janelle continued. "Take your time and go slow. Honor your emotions and don't blame yourself. Think of what you are doing as connecting too and living for Melanie."

I took a deep breath in and then let it out.

"Jayd," Janelle said softly. I felt a hand on my leg. "I don't want you to move too quickly if you aren't ready. Take this slow. This is a great first step."

I nodded, and turned my head towards Janelle's desk, looking past it and at the window behind. It was a clear day today. Warm, and crowded on the streets below. Janelle's room was filled with the scent of lavender incense.

"So, what's the first thing you will attempt in finding out more about Melanie?" Janelle asked.

I pondered this question for a bit as I glanced at her.

She wore a pretty, yellow, ruffled, silk blouse and a pair of matching capris and heels. She had on dangly sparkly earrings and a matching necklace.

"I guess...I could look her up more online. Look up her social media, where she went to school and worked. Friends and family of her's…"

It was really all I could initially think of. It wasn't like I could afford to hire a private investigator to research the life of Melanie.

"Good!" Janelle exclaimed. "That's a good start."

"Look into her social media and see if you can grasp any insight into her personal and social life. I'm sure you'll find out about many things, Jayd."

Janelle went on and on about what type of things I could find and where I could look. I listened and also drifted away, thinking about my plan in action.

I told Janelle I wanted to look into the life of Melanie so that I could finally face the woman whose life I undoubtedly ruined, and to get some type of closure from it all.

What I didn't tell Janelle was that I planned on doing and being everything, Melanie was.

Her very essence. What she liked and disliked. What she thought about and what she lived and hoped for. Her daily life and the things she aspired to be. Her secrets, her spouse, and her job.

All of it.

And most of all I wanted to complete the life of the woman I caused to die.

Molly sat on Janelle's desk. She was looking a little haggard, like she hadn't slept in a few days. Dark circles lined her eyes as she peered at Janelle's front door, looking away from us. I wonder what she was thinking. Or could she even think at all?

I wanted to get started on my plan as soon as possible.

Looking into Melanie's social media would be the easy part. Deciphering and analyzing every word and every picture she posted would be the challenge.

I don't want to know that you smiled in that picture, Melanie. I want to know what made you smile.

I thought this to myself as I focused back on Janelle.

"I don't want you to overwhelm yourself, Jayd. Take your time. Inch by inch, let yourself into Melanie's life. I bet you'll find that she wasn't much different than yourself."

Yeah...right.

Melanie and I were as alike as a slice of pizza and a flashlight. Not even made up of the same compounds.

Melanie's aura, just by looking at her, was similar to Mama's. Charismatic, energetic, beautiful, and beloved by many.

I'm sure Melanie fit into the puzzle that life was. Effortlessly.

I felt a slight bit of excitement, and yet strangely hopeless and fearful all at the same time. I tried not to look at Janelle, and instead looked back out the window behind her desk. The window was wide open, letting in some air. Pigeons flew in the sky, and cars angrily honked as their drivers shouted. Breezes fluttered Janelle's curtains and they drifted in the air. The scent of vanilla filled my nostrils. Vanilla and...orange? I wasn't sure exactly, but I liked the smell.

Janelle seemed to like fruit and plant scents. I wonder what scents Melanie liked. From her photos in news articles, she looked like a spice and nature type of scent. A cool ocean breeze or freshly rained forest mixed with cinnamon and nutmeg. A warm and natural presence.

God...why? Why did I have to do that to her? Why did she have to be there? Why did she...

I felt a pair of eyes on me. I glanced over at Janelle and sure enough, she was staring intently at me. I looked away. Once again, it was unsettling. I'm used to gazing and analyzing people. Not the other way around.

It wasn't just not being the right puzzle piece. The touch and go of the world and the inner turmoil of it all hang heavy on me. The callousness of it all. Every aching scream and shout for someone passing by to stop and listen and acknowledge how this all just wasn't right. That something was wrong. With each of us. With our environment. With the whole fucking world.

Why was it only I who felt this?

Not even when there was silence did they pay attention. Look around and ask themselves. What was the purpose of it all? And why? No one cared. Why?

I didn't want to be a part of it. The drumming in my head, the disgusting complicity in it all. The staring and tension everywhere. Why couldn't anyone understand, or maybe, just acknowledge that it was all wrong? But instead, we go along with it, like puppets on a string, like a dog pulled away from its wonders on a leash. We go along with it and we accept it until someone snaps. Until someone breaks down. Until someone becomes dangerous. Until someone can no longer go on and wants out.

So, I didn't want any part of it anymore. The whole world could be swallowed and all lost and it wouldn't matter one bit to me.

No, I wasn't going to use violence and take others with me wherever I was going. I was happily leaping away from them to get to this place. Goodbye, shitty world. Why did you ever exist and what was the point of it all?

And in the torment of myself and the ever-yielding emotions that I would undoubtedly succumb to if I held it in, I cried, letting the tears spill softly down my cheek and drip off of my chin.

Janelle watched me, saying nothing and something with her gaze at the same time.

Chapter 12

Looking up at the large, brown, doe-like eyes looking down into my own, I gritted my teeth and looked away. It was scary sometimes, looking into the face that matched mine as it stared back at me. The eyes that were my own, but on the face of a being I hated.

I lay on my bed as Molly, bent over the side of the bed, stared down at me.

I don't know how long she was standing there as she appeared at any and all times. This time it started when I opened my eyes and saw my face, like a mirror, looking back.

She seemed...agitated.

Aggressive.

She had been acting like that for a while now.

Norman was sleeping beside me. His murmurs filled the silence between my mirror image and I. R&B music played in the background. The song that was playing now had such a rhythmic chorus. Sylvia played the same song today when I stayed after.

I really didn't want to look at her, much less acknowledge that she was here. Both psychically here now, or theoretically evening existing.

Molly had been a part of my life for as long as I can remember. Her origin is a mystery. She just appeared one day and it was as if she had always been there. Exactly when she came, I do not remember. That part of my memory has always been clouded. I do know, however, that I hate her, and that she appeared only to annoy and torment me.

Whenever I fell down and injured myself when I was younger or when I got in trouble and received a scolding from Mama and would cry, Molly would be there, smirking or laughing at me.

Whenever I fucked up or did something I shouldn't have done, Molly was there to make me feel guilty and unrepentable.

I could do nothing right in her eyes even when everything I did was right. I was always wrong, bad, a liar, ugly, miserable, unwanted, and alone. She would often try to invoke me into violence or outbursts.

Molly always reminded me that I was alone in the world.

Molly looks like me. Exactly like me.

As I grew, so did she. As my body developed and cuts and bruises made their permanent marks, and lines and creases set into my youth, so did Molly's. She was I and I was she.

Only, she didn't dress like me.

She wore little sun dresses that reminded me of the ones that I wore when I was very young. It looked silly on her and she was so overgrown in them, yet that was all she wore. Tiny little sundresses in every color of the rainbow. She also wore matching bows and ribbons in her hair, like a little girl. It was strange, and made me uncomfortable.

But everything about Molly made me uncomfortable and confused. Like, why was she even here? And where did she come from? What was her purpose?

I could never analyze Molly like I would everyday people. For anytime I tried, Molly would just reflect myself back on to me. When I peered at her she would peer back at me. Similar emotions radiated off of her as they did me. She was not only imitating my appearance, but also what I felt inside. But the feelings didn't feel right. Molly felt corrupted.

When trying to analyze her, she would block me or turn away when I stared for too long. Sometimes she would disappear altogether. Other times, she would scare me by shouting when it was quiet or appearing when I looked up. She would laugh, as if this was punishment for trying to figure her out.

What do you want? It was the question I would ask her over and over again. I would scream it out, mumble it in my sleep, or state it when I felt her nearby. She, of course, never answered.

It was like she knew I was trying to get in and she would do all she could do to keep me out.

And she was cruel. Oh, how Molly could be so cruel to me.

I wasn't smart nor did I have any friends. How pathetic.

My birthdays were her favorite day because I was one year older and closer to death.

I wasn't as pretty as Mama, and never would be. That hurt the least though, as I had long accepted this.

And the laughing and sneering and mocking. And the staring. It never stopped.

I don't think Molly has ever said one nice thing to me.

No one ever saw Molly of course. Only I did. Which made it all the worse, because I couldn't report Molly for stalking or harassment; she didn't exist in the world. Only mine.

I didn't dare tell Mama about Molly. She would truly freak out and I was too old for imaginary friends. But Molly wasn't a friend. She wasn't even exactly an enemy.

Molly was always the dark entity that lived on the outer edges of my imagination and the little secret forcing her way into my reality. I tolerated her, though I had no choice. She wouldn't go away. I would never accept her.

For whatever her existence meant, I felt that it was far scarier and more tragic than what it appeared to be.

Chapter 13

It was exactly how I'd imagine it would be. She was surrounded by dozens of friends and family members. A large social following, smiling with her partner in beautiful locations around the world. Lavish parties and chic fashion. There were quotes with thousands of likes, updates on the progression of goals and dreams. Loving photos with her partner. I saw a graduation picture and forced myself to not look away. Both of her parents were on either side of her, holding each of her hands. They looked so proud. I knew it would be like this, but my heart felt as if it would sink into my stomach at any moment.

This was my first glimpse into the life of Melanie as I scrolled through her online profile.

A beautiful, brown skinned woman with bright eyes and a gorgeous smile looked back at me in a profile picture. She had clear, perfect skin, and white teeth. Her nose was small, her lashes were long, and her eyes were like a Baby doll's- large, innocent, and full of wonder.

This was the face of the woman whose life I took by what I attempted.

Mama and Aunt Opal were out today and I would be going into work later. Mama left a note saying that they wouldn't be back until late evening. They probably were going to a friend's gathering or trip. I was never asked if I wanted to go, nor did I want to. The apartment was nice and quiet and I liked being alone. I was used to it by now. Who wants to hang out with older folks anyway?

Mclanic...

I looked below her profile picture at her description. It was italicized.

Melanie Medela. 25. Elated new Medical School student. Future Wife to a Wonderful Future Husband.

Medela. Melanie's last name was Medela.

Why hadn't I known that?

It was odd, but I had never focused on the fact that Melanie had a last name.

Was I just blocking it out?

I continued to scroll through her profile.

I stopped when I saw him.

If there ever was an epitome of tall, dark, and handsome, he would be it. I knew right away he was Melanie's partner. In the photo posted of him, he had on shades and a baseball cap, but I could still make out his features. The caption below read: Mr. Cool.

There was a comment from Melanie above his photo. *My amazing husband Paul. You are the light of my world and have always been my number one fan!*

My eyes averted downward and I scrolled even further down. I was hit with it like a punch to the face. Thousands of messages on their condolences, their sorrows, shocks and pain at the death of Melanie.

The world has lost an amazing person! One comment read.

I can't believe you're gone! This isn't real. Said another.

In complete shock! How could this have happened! One person wrote.

I'm so sorry, Melanie. Gone too soon. Poor Paul! Said some else.

Numbness fell over my body. I stopped looking at the screen and looked down at my hands.

Why had I thought this would have been a good idea, again? How could I ever live up to someone that was so beloved and apparently full of life and energy?

Because you always want to be the victim, Jayd

Molly's voice made me jump as I sat on my bed with my laptop on my legs.

My eyes quickly shot back to my computer screen. Molly was somewhere in front of me but I didn't dare look up. My hands continued to scroll. After a minute of aimlessly scrolling, something caught my eye.

On the right hand side of the screen, I saw a promotion for an upcoming marathon this weekend. It was for animal abuse and adoption awareness and was a joint effort with shelters from across the state to raise funds.

Many people commented below about their excitement to join. I quickly scrolled up and clicked on messages and posts made by Melanie and sure enough, she had commented on the promotion late last year.

Can't wait to attend! Got my running shoes!

I closed my laptop, hopped off my bed, grabbed my bag and headed out to buy new sneakers that I couldn't afford.

Chapter 14

"You know I never bothered to find out what her last name was. It was Medela"

"Yes, Jayd. I noticed that," Janelle spoke through the phone as I sat in the grass, shaded by a large tree. "I have a theory for why you didn't, but it's understandable. Anyway, I'm glad you're doing this. Make sure you drink plenty of water and take a break if you have to."

She sounded relaxed as she spoke. I imagined that she was laying down on the couch or sitting back in her chair at her desk with her feet up. And a cup of tea nearby.

The sun's rays drifted through the spaces between the leaves. It was the beginning of August and had cooled down from the previous summer month. I exhaled as a slight breeze went by.

My back leaned into the base of the large tree. I had to be careful not to drift off and fall asleep because I was in such comfort. There was no one around because I had gotten to the park very early before the marathon began. I let out a huge yawn.

"I have like three water bottles, my music, and a portable charger. I'm good."

Though I said it, in the back of my head I couldn't ignore the anxiety that was brewing in my stomach and chest and worst of all, my mind. I had never run in a marathon and to be honest, never ran around amongst a group of people in public. Not even in my school days did I run in PE, and would often sit on the gym floor by the bleachers, waiting until the clock ticked along and class was over. But I knew that didn't matter and I had to shove these thoughts and feelings aside today. I was here and committed to this.

I looked down at my feet, briefly admiring the new running shoes I bought. They were purple and gray. Two of my favorite colors.

I knew I was wasting money on them and the donation I had given to marathon organizers, but I had to go through with it. For Melanie. And besides, I liked animals. Better than humans sometimes.

I pulled my jacket around my shoulders and turned back to Janelle on the phone. She had still been talking about how pleased and eager she was for me to begin this journey. I politely interrupted her.

"Janelle?"

"Yes, Jayd?"

"What did you mean by having a theory on why I didn't acknowledge Melanie's last name?" I asked, truly wanting to know. It intrigued me the second she said it.

There was a brief silence before I heard a soft sigh. I knew this to mean that she would be picking her words carefully, but telling me the truth.

"Well, Jayd," Janelle began. "Given the trauma and guilt that you're facing, I believe that you, perhaps subconsciously as opposed to deliberately, tried to minimize humanizing Melanie. And by this, I mean that instead of Melanie being this whole living being that was once here, she is instead, this figure that is personified by a past incident that you need to move away from and hide away forever."

Her words hit like a bolder to the gut. What was she saying??

As if to answer my question, Janelle continued.

"I do believe that if you kept on this path, Jayd, you would eventually liken Melanie's to a fable to help ease your guilt, never taking the responsibility of facing your past, and, well, forget Melanie altogether."

"Think of it as a fairytale. Look at the old fairytale books that we read when we're children. Notice few have last names, with some even having names such as Sleeping Beauty or Snow White. They're mystical and dreamy. We love and cherish their happy ending stories, but we acknowledge that they are fictional, that their names are not traditional or normal, and that life is not a fairytale. They are a way for us to escape, but we cannot completely humanize them like we do to each other. They, and their stories, are the beauty and purity that we see lacking in the world. They are almost flawless, their essence being unattainable for most. We see them, love their stories, but know that they are not real nor do they fully encompass what we believe it means to be a human being."

"Did they ever go through painful periods and develop cramps? What was their first sexual experience? How did they feel being women in their times? Does life really get better instantly after a prince comes and save you? Maybe. Maybe not."

"Those questions are considered inappropriate nor are they relevant to their stories. They are here as a form of entertainment, escape, and believing in dreams coming true. Nothing more."

"So yes, Jayd. I did believe that you would attempt to forget Melanie and liken what happened to just being a bad dream that you had to eventually wake up from. Like a fairytale plot of being poisoned or cursed and that you would simply have to wait until someone comes and saves you. But it doesn't work that way, Jayd. When I first met you, you were showing signs of dissonance. Which, in my experience with my patients, leads to gaslighting their trauma and then complete dejection of the events."

"That wall in your mind has to be broken down, Jayd. When you shut out things that hurt or cause you to think about that hurt, you prevent yourself from truly healing and coming to terms with what happened."

I didn't say anything. Was I too stunned? My mind was thinking of a million things, but nothing at all. Was I hurt by what she said? By the truth or by the reality of it? Around me the environment seemed to close in, yet expand.

Did I really just want to forget about Melanie and what happened?

"Jayd...?"

Janelle'e voice snapped me back into reality and I realized that I hadn't responded to her.

It was pretty cool right now outside with a light breeze, but heat was brewing inside of me. I respected Janelle, but I wanted some time to think.

"Janelle, I have to go. They're about to start so I'll call you afterwards." I hung up before she could respond.

Sinking my back into the base of the tree even further, I laid my head completely backwards and closed my eyes. I exhaled deeply.

It felt like every cell in my body was going off like fireworks. In the distance I could hear cars driving by, birds chirping, and people shouting. The air around me was congested and polluted, yet I knew this park was one of the closest things to nature in this concrete city.

Without opening my eyes, I slipped my phone into my bag that laid beside me on the grass and I dug my hands into the Earth. I wish I could be one with it. Funnily enough, months ago I was close to being buried far beneath it.

But Melanie was beneath it.

She's worm food now. Because of you.

Molly's voice interjected my thoughts. Why couldn't this bitch just leave me alone? Maybe she's a demon, here to torture me.

Taking my hands out of the ground, I reached behind me and felt the bark of the tree. It was hard and tough, but I liked the feeling of it. I wonder how old this tree was? It could be thousands of years old. I wonder how much it experienced throughout all of those years. The stories it could tell. The life that vibrated up through its roots all those years.

I wonder what it would be like to be a tree? Would it be better to be a tree than me?

Of course, it would. Being dirt itself would be better than being you, Jayd.

Molly's words stung me like a bee. I didn't open my eyes to look where she was. I did what I do best whenever Molly spoke to me. It was the one place she couldn't get to me outside of Pat's. Breathing in deeply and exhaling, I drifted off to sleep, hoping some bum wouldn't come by and rob me.

This was a tactic I would use whenever I got into trouble with Mama, whatever Aunt Opal was berating me, or whenever Molly started harassing me. I drifted off into a light sleep, feeling the vibrations and noise around me while blocking out their voices.

Minutes painfully passed by as if they were hours and the voices of people grew louder. I was sure participants and spectators would be spilling into the park soon.

Well Jayd, there's no turning back now. Open your eyes and wake up.

I could feel the heat and hear the motion of many feet shuffling into the park. Was it almost time? More minutes passed by and it felt like an eternity before I heard a distant horn and the voice of a woman pierce through the murmurs of the crowds.

"Hey you!" she shouted. "Up there! Are you running today?"

My eyes shot open and I jumped up in an instant, staggering to my feet. Standing far off down a hill in front of me was a heavyset Black woman. She wore a navy tracksuit and had a clipboard in her hand.

"We're about to begin!" she said, waving up to me. "Are you participating?"

"Yes!" I yelled down to her.

"Well, you need to come down here and get a number. Everyone running needs a number. Let's go!"

I hastily grabbed my bag and headed for the main entrance. As I got over the hill I was taken aback by the hordes of people. There were many more people than I thought there would be. It seemed like there had to at least be a thousand people just in my peripheral view.

Were all these people running? I thought to myself.

Break a leg, Jayd. Both of them.

I ignored Molly and followed the woman to the park's gate. There were several other men and women behind a table and a stack of large stickers with numbers on them.

"Here," the woman said, bending down to take a sticker and handing it to me. "Stick it on your chest, arm, stomach, back...wherever. It just needs to be visible. Walk up to the front up there and wait. We're going to begin in five minutes."

I did as she said and placed the sticker onto my chest. Without looking anyone in the eye, I walked straight through the crowds, weaving in and out of the chatter, laughter, and shouting. We would be running laps around the park. There were chairs on the sidewalks and I could now see that the streets were marked off with police at each corner.

"Ladies and gentlemen, we're going to begin in five minutes!" a male's voice bellowed in a microphone. "Those of you participating please get ready! Those of you here to cheer them on, please step aside and give the runners room!"

I walked briskly until I got to the front of the line, stopping right behind it. With my bag across my torso, I stuffed my hands into my jacket pockets. Okay Melanie, I'm here for you. This is what you would have liked. Running for a great cause. What an amazing person you must have been.

The streets began to fill up with the runners centering themselves and many observers filtered out onto the sidewalk. The minutes must have gone by like seconds because I heard the sound of the horn again, this time accompanied by the shouting of the same woman who called to me earlier.

"Alright! Here we go!" she shouted from behind. "Countdown in ten! Runners take your place!"

I took my hands out of my pockets and looked forward. I was by no means the best runner in the world, but sprinting was as easy as pie. It wasn't the running that made me anxious, or even the many people that had gathered around. I felt something was off. The presence of someone. My heartbeat was beginning to pick up again.

And then it completely stopped.

Wait. Why was I in the very front? This was the absolute worst place to be! So much attention would be drawn to me! What if I tripped or something? I'd be trampled and humiliated by everyone else!

I knew I realized this too late when I heard the echoes of a countdown and saw the mile long crowds of people standing on the sidelines.

"Eight...nine...ten...let's go!"

Fearing potentially bumping into someone if I stood still, I began to sprint at full speed. At least no one would look me in the eye and only see me from behind.

I kept an easy and steady pace ahead of the others. My eyes stayed glued to the path in front of me as shops and people drifted behind me. A few minutes into the marathon, I slowly began to feel less anxious.

See Jayd? This isn't so bad.

I wonder if Melanie liked to jog? Not just in a marathon, but in general. In her photos that I saw online, she looked quite fit and healthy. No doubt she would be side by side with me out here. I was not exactly fit, but I could always manage to sprint nicely.

In the corner of my eye, I saw the movement of someone running on the far edge near the sidewalk. Their movements were erratic and clumsy. And they were flapping their arms like...a bird. I glanced over in confusion, and then quickly glanced back in frustration.

It was Molly, and she was exaggeratedly imitating my sprinting. She kept up with me effortlessly. She was my mirror image, after all.

More minutes passed and I was beginning the second lap around the park. People on the sidewalks on either side cheered all of us runners on, and I got a small warm feeling from it all. This wasn't bad at all, I thought. I had been worried for nothing.

And then I saw him and I choked. Like a punch in the face or an on-coming crash, I braced myself. Dozens of emotions in one erupted and I almost tripped over my feet. Sprinting at a rapid pace right past me on my left was...him again.

He sprinted past me and I couldn't get a glimpse of his face, but I knew it was him. On his back was the number 069.

Oh god, no. No! He can't be here! Why here? Why now? Shit! Fuck!

Quickly grabbing my hoodie I pulled it over my head and pulled in the strings, concealing my face.

Don't turn around. Please don't turn around! I hope he didn't notice me when he ran up from behind.... I need to get the hell out of here!

Without wasting any time, I eased off towards the right side of the street and looked for an opening in the crowds. When I saw one at the corner of the street I made a break for it, making sure to hide my face from him. In seconds I had broken through the crowd and exited the marathon.

"Hey!? Where are you going?" I could hear someone shout from the crowd, but I was long down the street, zooming towards home. I didn't dare turn around for fear that he would spot me.

Minutes went by and soon I was running up my apartment stairs and through the hallways and into our apartment. I burst through my door and stopped, relieved, and caught my breath.

I looked up, and sitting on my bed was Molly. She looked at me and smiled.

Chapter 15

"Shut the door on your way out! You left it ajar yesterday! Sylvia's voice drifted over to me as I made my way to the front of the store's door, preparing to leave for the day. I had spent the second half of the afternoon stocking and cleaning shelves. I would come back later in the evening to do some sweeping. Tomorrow I'll work overtime again. It was dusty and mundane work, but the money was desperately needed since my medical bills wouldn't pay themselves. Mama was still making calls, but it was looking more and more hopeless that they would give us any extension. The first major payment was due in two weeks.

"Ok, I will!" I called back to Sylvia. I grabbed my bag and skipped to the front door and left the store, shutting the door tightly.

It was beautiful outside today. Not too cool, clouds were sparse and the sun was shining brightly.

I walked over towards my rented bike that was chained to a light post and began to unlock it. It was a nice, purple, mountain bike. I would be biking today before I head home and then back to work later.

Something else I found out from Melanie's profile was that she liked to bike all throughout the city.

I wonder if Melanie liked the city, or if she just lived and worked here because of the opportunities? That's what I often felt from the expats living in New York City. They loved what New York could offer, but not New York in itself. After a few weeks that glistening wonder in their eyes would fade away. The lights, the noise, the crowds and the smells would become familiar, and to some extent, they would start to become an annoyance. I had a love-hate relationship with New York. I loved

Harlem, despite it not being the Harlem of that past, but I hated the greater New York feel. It made me queasy. The people, the rudeness, the directness. It was all so suffocating. I don't know, however, where I would go if I ever left New York.

I was Jayd Broussard, the unusual and unremarkable daughter of the beautiful and charismatic Ruby Broussard. Who would I be if not that? The very thought perplexed, yet frightened me. There was comfort in the notion that I had an identity. I'd be completely lost if I wasn't the girl I knew.

Unlocking my bike I clamped the chain underneath the bike, pushed back the kickstand, swung my leg over the seat and pushed off.

I flew down the street, block after block, dodging people walking their dogs, sitting outdoor dining or simply walking. At each corner I stopped and observed my surroundings.
People walking, talking and glancing in a pass and go way. I rode on.

Speeding down the streets, the wind blew through my hair and cooled my skin. My bag slapped against my side whenever I hit a crack or bump.

I don't know where I was going, or if I was going anywhere at all. I just wanted to ride and let the minutes pass by. Grumbles erupted from my stomach. Damn. I haven't eaten since breakfast and it was well past noon. I looked at the stores and food trucks all around me. I could easily just buy something and snack on it for a bit.

I eyed and pulled over to a chicken and burger shop and locked my bike to a bike post just outside of it.

Running into the store, I ordered a small burger and a diet Coke. The store worker was a cute, young Black girl, perhaps only a few years older than me.

"Are you dining in?" she asked me.

"No," I told her. "To go please"

In a few minutes my order was given to me in a white bag. I paid the girl and headed out. Putting my food in my bag, I unlocked and hopped back on my bike, riding on.

I went speeding past laughing and curious children and their mothers scolding or holding their hands.

What did Melanie do when she biked around New York City? Did she admire nature and the people around? The infrastructure, the stores, or the traffic?

I was now miles from home and right beside me, sprawling to my right, was one of many of New York's parks. I could see young men playing basketball and others watching them. Why not eat lunch at the park today Jayd, I thought to myself. It's a nice day, and Molly hasn't appeared to bother me yet. Let's enjoy the moment before we head home. I rode across the street to the park. I'll watch the basketball game and relax. When I reached the park entrance, I rode in and stopped, gazing around until I could spot a bench to sit down at.

I spotted something else.

He stood only a few feet away from me this time, and I could fully make out his handsome features. Chiseled jaw and long lashes. He had dimples as well. He was jogging it would seem, as he wore shorts and running shoes. He had a bottle of water in his hand and seemed to have paused to gulp it down. In his ears were headphones. He was directly to my right and hadn't seen me ride up.

No. No fucking way. Out of all of Manhattan...just how? Just how do we meet again?

It was him again. Like a bad memory that continued to pop up again and again and overwhelmed me. Was fate playing a joke on me? Of course, it was. It always was. At least he hadn't seen me.

Until he did.

As if to torment me further, fate decided to have him look directly my way. Honey eyes latched onto mine. I froze for a moment, and then blinked and pulled my eyes away.

Whirling my bike around, I sped out of the park and headed home.

Before I could stop myself, I looked back, half expecting him to be behind me. He was now at the park entrance, watching me ride off. I turned around and picked up my pace. His face...his expression. He looked concerned.

Chapter 16

Ouch.

Whoever said yoga was supposed to be relaxing, lied. I think I might have pulled something.
Arms and legs stretched out on a towel, I laid on my stomach. Then I rolled around on my back, exhaling deeply.
Melanie would often do yoga with friends and sign up for yoga and fitness classes. Since I had neither friends nor would I dare be in a closed room embarrassing myself in front of strangers, I decided to do some yoga back at the park I biked to earlier. Whatever maneuver I made on my stomach with my back leg pulled up went terribly wrong. A sharp pain emitted from my back and upper thigh. Laying on my back now, I continued breathing in and out heavily. Molly was nearby or arriving soon. I felt her presence growing stronger, as my anxiety grew. It was always the same feelings before she would emerge, and I dreaded it but knew that it was unavoidable. It was time for me to go anyway, I had been at this for an hour. Very slowly I pulled my body in and got to my feet. Pain shot through my entire left side.

Hehehehe

I heard her before I saw her. Keeping my eyes focused on gathering my things and not searching for where she was, I tried to stand up and make my way out of the park. I felt restless...or rather that was the feelings that I was picking up around me. As I made my way to the park entrance, I saw people hurriedly exiting and entering the park. I spotted a young boy with his mom. He was racing towards the playground and pulling his mother along as she objected. Right next to the park entrance was an ice cream cart and, in the street, right next to it was a hotdog truck. My stomach grumbled. I had lunch a few hours earlier, and Mama was cooking tonight and I didn't want to spoil dinner. It was almost three o'clock in the afternoon and I had been at the park since noon.

I walked out of the park and made a left. A dark presence followed me and it wasn't my shadow. Molly was close by, trailing me. My left side still ached, but I wanted to get home and lie down so I kept walking. Droplets of sweat poured down from my head and my body felt sore. Intense yoga was not for me. The human body wasn't made to stretch and twist into so many positions.
I wonder how Melanie did it? She probably made it look effortless in the pictures I saw in her online photo album.

I continued to walk down the street, heading home. When I got there, I would jump straight into the shower and then to bed. To my right, cars and trucks honked at each other and zigged zagged through traffic. It was after lunch and people were probably headed back to work or to pick up their kids from school.

I wonder what it would be like to have kids? I wonder if Melanie wanted kids? Did she want a boy or a girl? Maybe even twins. Maybe she only wanted one child or perhaps a dozen. Who knew? Only she did and her partner did.

And you took that possibility away from them, Jayd.

Molly's words hurt worse than a first-degree burn. Her words simmered in the air like smoke, and floated over me with each inhale. It was beginning to suffocate me. And she didn't stop.

Why, why did you do it, Jayd? You ruined their lives. You might as well have held her head under water yourself. So selfish of you. You shouldn't be here, and you know it.

Did I know it? Life was like a blur sometimes. Days passed by and I could be eating and sleeping and thinking but sometimes it didn't even seem real. Like a machine.

You're worse than a machine, Jayd. At least a machine has a purpose. Why are you even alive? You don't deserve to be.

Was I even alive? There were times I half expected to wake up and find out that I had actually drowned and Melanie was still here. That I had been going through this world in a sort of purgatory spirit state. That I would realize that I had been dead all along. That maybe this was even all a dream. Or a nightmare.

But every day I would wake up. Still here, and still reminded of what happened.

It did happen. Jayd. And you'll be reminded of it until the day you die. You will never know peace.

I kept walking. Taking a quick look around, I realized that I hadn't gone very far; not even a block from the park. My left side was now screaming in agony. The muscles felt as if they were torn. Throbs of pain shot up my entire side so intensely that it was unbearable. I couldn't make it home like this. I needed to sit down.

I quickly glanced around for any bench or shop that I could sit down at. Up at the next block, I spotted a small cafe. I took off towards the cafe while squeezing my left side and ignoring the horrific pain. Hurriedly crossing the street and running up to the entrance, I shot inside and sat down at the first empty table.

Baby steps, I told myself. This wasn't an ideal activity in terms of fulfilling Melanie's wishes and being her as much as possible, but beggars couldn't be choosers. Melanie's family had taken over much of her social media, and quite a bit of information was blocked to and limited to only those she had chosen to follow. Yoga and jogging couldn't be all there was to Melanie Medela. From the comments on her profile, I could tell that she was a very outgoing, generous, and intelligent person. I had barely scratched the surface.

Maybe hiring a private detective wasn't such a bad idea after all.

Just give up, Jayd. Give up. You have no idea what you're doing. Pathetic. Melanie would laugh in your face.

Molly's words pricked me like a splinter.

And then there was what happened yesterday.

It was still beating me up inside; ringing out my guts. No amount of mediation and yoga today would help. Maybe that was what this awful cramp in my left side was about and not the yoga.
I had been online on one of Melanie's more popular social media profiles. I wanted to ask some of her followers questions and I had begun by complimenting Melanie and then ending my compliments in a question, hoping her relatives or close friends would fill in the blanks.

They did. I wish they hadn't.

I scanned through Melanie's available photos and spotted one where she was pictured with two women, smiling, and they all had their arms around each other. Finding their profiles, I further saw photos of Melanie with the women. Confident that they were most likely all friends, I searched for messages left by them on Melanie's profile.

After Melanie died, a memorial post was left on her page. Most likely created by her family, it honored the life and legacy of Melanie. In the memorial photo, a beautiful Melanie was smiling with straight, white teeth and surrounded by a border of flowers. Below her photo was not hundreds, but thousands of comments of sorrow and remembrance by all who knew her. As I skimmed through the comments, it felt like my heart was being squeezed. Melanie was so popular and loved. Everyone missed her and said the world lost a great person. Things would never be the same.

"RIP Mel! You were such a bright light in my life. Gone too soon!"

"I can't believe you're gone. It just isn't fair! I miss you so much!"

"Rest easy, Melanie! You were a wonderful person!"

Every word of every message was like a dagger to the heart.

What had I done? Why did I do it?

After a few moments of pondering my eyes caught a familiar face. It was one of Melanie's friends that she had been pictured with. A red-headed, blued eyed, freckled woman. Her message had thousands of likes. It was the highest rated comment on the post.

"Melanie, you were like a sister. We met in college and from the first time we saw each other, I knew we would forever be best friends. You supported me through the years while succeeding at your own career. I simply cannot come to terms with the fact that you are no longer here. That your young life was cut short due to some selfish idiot. They should be the one gone, not you! You were always such a cheery and kind person. Why does life take the good ones away? I hope the girl who you selflessly saved is tormented everyday of her life. I hope she feels the pain that all your loved ones feel. She has no idea she took away someone so amazing from this world. You had some much more to accomplish. You will always be remembered. RIP, Mel!"

My eyes were glued to the computer screen. Minutes went by, but they felt like hours. I read the message again and again. I read it silently and aloud. I read it backwards, I read every other line, and I read it until I couldn't read it anymore. My eyes were watering but they stayed glued to the screen. I didn't bother blinking. It wouldn't matter if I did. I couldn't unsee what was written. The sting of dryness from my lack of blinking became painful, but I couldn't force myself to cry. I couldn't force the tears out and give my eyes some relief. I don't know why, but I tortured myself as I sat there staring at the screen. Maybe I thought I deserved it.

You do deserve it Jayd, you do. You deserve it all. All of the pain. All of the torment. All of the humiliation. And you know it.

Was that Molly speaking?

I guess it didn't matter. It could easily be myself talking to myself. I decided not to message Melanie's friend. Or any person that she was close to. I had shut my computer off after that and forgot what I had done for the rest of the day. It had really all been a blur.

The cafe I sat at was quite noisy and crowded. It had a vintage 70's aesthetic with roller skates and a pair of bell bottoms decorating the wall and a large disco ball hanging from the wall in the middle of the room. I flicked through the menu on the table and saw that it was a vegan cafe. The cramped pain to my side was drowning out my hunger, but I needed to rest here before heading home. I would order something light so as not to spoil dinner. I settled on a tofu wrap and a diet coke.

The pain at my left side diminished a bit and my heart beat had slowed as I leaned back against my chair and breathed in and out. Young adults were spread out amongst the tables and I could see a second floor with additional seating. 70's classics played and I nodded along to the music. This atmosphere was relaxed and laughter and chattering buzzed everywhere around me.

Molly danced in the middle of the room, twirling around and around. I watched as people walked and looked right through her. She danced ridiculously as she looked over at me with a wide grin. If there was one thing I was envious about pertaining to Molly, it was the fact that she was invisible to the world around her. Free to be a buffoon with no one watching.

No one except me.

The music continued to drift throughout the room and I caught a server looking my way and motioning to me that she'll be over in a second. I patiently waited for a server to come take my order. I wished she would hurry up. The aroma of spices, weed, and some flowery fragrance filled my nostrils. The front door to the cafe swung open and a couple walked in. One girl had brightly colored green hair and her girlfriend had multiple facial piercings. They held each other's hands tightly as they spoke to the hostess. At that moment I had realized that I had not even been seated, and had run into this cafe and sat at the first place I saw. The hostess hadn't said a word to me.

"Table for two, please!" the one with the piercings said to the hostess. She smiled at them and gestured for them to follow her as she grabbed two menus underneath her booth. I watched them as they walked by my table, wondering how they met. Who came out first? Who pronounced their love to the other first? Were they the same age and when did they meet?

Ten minutes had come and gone. Molly had stopped dancing and was now sitting beside me, looking down at a menu. I watched as she ran her finger along the words and prices, mouthing something. Several servers were cleaning up a table to my right and out of the back side to my left, a server came out with a large tray of food. Somewhere up ahead a female voice squealed, followed by an eruption of laughter. A heavy sigh escaped my lips. In addition to being anxiety ridden, I had come to know myself as a severe introvert. Public settings either made my skin crawl or drained me. Today it was the latter. The couple was now nearly out of view, but I could see them being sat far off in the back of the cafe.

The bell to the restaurant's front door rang, indicating that someone had just come in. "I'll be right there!" call the hostess as she began jogging back towards the front.

Glancing away from the couple, I began to watch Molly again. As the hostess made her way to the front, my eyes followed her, looking to see who had just come in. I almost bit through my tongue as I had been completely unaware that he had walked in and had been watching me.

Yet again, it was him. Tall, dark, broad shoulders, and handsome him. He was gorgeous...and sweating. As if he had just finish working out. How long ago had he walked in and how long he had been glancing my way, I don't know.

All I know is that when our eyes met, panic washed over me, my throat tightened and my heart stopped. It was like the fear you get when you are moments away from being hit by a train. The mere moments right before the impact.

In a blinding flurry I was out the cafe door, passing him, and not believing my luck could be this bad.

Chapter 17

"Hello everyone, my name is Candie! It's nice to meet you all!" shouted the lanky, flamboyant, young man as he stood up abruptly.

Loud snickers erupted from the room. It was time to introduce ourselves and Candie had taken it upon himself to be first. We sat in a large circle of chairs in a brightly lit room facing the key speaker, the cliche group discussion setting you would see in every drama film. There was of course the wise guy or clown of the group and Candie was the person.

"Um, thank you Candie!" the director, a short, frail man said as he gestured for Candie to sit down. "But I would like to call on each of you to speak and introduce yourselves--- if that's ok with you?"

More snickering.

Candie looked around at all of us. His expression had been initial shock, and then embarrassment, followed by hurt and disgruntlement. Dejected, he sat back down in a huff, arms and legs crossed, and head hanging towards the floor.

There were about fifty of us in this group and I was sitting on the far edge of the circle, as far away from the others as possible. Tilting back into my chair, my eyes skimmed the many faces in the room. Young, old, rough, and depressed were the words that came to mind. Candie stood out like ink on white paper. His brightly colored pink pantsuit with ruffles at all ends was an eyesore. He was tall. Freakishly tall and had dyed white-blonde hair. His face was handsome though, against his mahogany skin.

A woman sat next to him and appeared to be the polar opposite. She wore a dark gray sweatsuit and sneakers with her gray hair tied into a bun. Her face was as wrinkled as a balled-up paper and her expression was sullen as she looked out at nothing with dead, glassy, eyes.

I wonder what her story would be. Recovering drug addict? Domestic violence victim? Or just a depressed, lonely old lady?

Her entire aura was gray and sad. Whatever was wrong with her and the reason for her being here, it had sucked the life out of her. She looked like a dead woman walking. I knew the feeling.
I wondered if this was her first time coming to these meetings. Maybe she had been to many and each time she got better. Or worse.

Candie on the other hand would be the lively and gay one. I wondered if he was an addict. Maybe he had HIV and was seeking support or maybe he had trouble accepting himself? He reminded me of a boy in high school who would flirt with guys at school, but act masculine around his parents. Someone told his dad about it one day and we never saw him afterwards. Later we learned that he ran away from home. I wondered where he was today.

But Candie seemed like he enjoyed the skin he was in. His energy and disposition were loud and proud. I was very interested in his story.

"Alright, we will begin now!" the director said as he stood up. He was so short and frail he could almost be mistaken for a child. It reminded me of Sylvia's height. Poor them.
"My name is Adam Wells and I am the director of Mental Health Matters. I'd like to thank you all for being here and frankly, I have to say, I'm impressed with the turnout. I see some old familiar faces, and I am very

pleased to see that you've returned. Today we have a volunteer assistant, Debra Gorden, and she will be here to help me run this meeting today."

Mr. Wells gestured towards a short haired, blond woman sitting beside him. She smiled as he said her name and looked down. Her feet were turned inwards and her hands were clasped.
Anxiety, I thought. She has anxiety. Brave of her to do this. It must be a part of her healing process in getting over her anxiety. My high school counselor suggested doing the same and going to social, public speaking events more to get over my anxiety. I never did, of course.

"We also had another volunteer, but it appears he decided not to come today. This program typically has two assistants helping me."

"No problem," he continued. "The show must go on and I'm sure Debra will do a great job helping out. I want everyone to unwind and relax. Again, thank you for coming."

Melanie often volunteered at this event. It was always short staffed, and it was one of her most charitable acts that was public on her social media profiles. She had dozens of photos with an entire room of people and her smiling in the middle. Today I would sit and observe and see if I could possibly volunteer. It was highly unlikely, but maybe like Debra, it was all a part of the healing process. And for Melanie, of course.

"Now, I'd like to call on each of you individually and ask you to introduce yourself to the group. Let's break the ice and get to know each other. We all come from different backgrounds and circumstances and I'm very happy that you all are here today to talk about it. Discussing our issues instead of keeping them bottled up or acting out negatively is one of the first steps to addressing our mental health issues."

"There is no judgment here!" Mr. Wells said. "We are all here to share and find comfort and support. Now, I don't want to pressure anyone to speak, but I would like to get to know you all. We will go around until each of you have gone, and then we'll break out into groups and have a fun session. How about that?"

Murmurs of agreement rumbled throughout the room which smelled like smoke, staleness and despair. The energies and auras of everyone felt like a one-thousand pound boulder on my shoulders. It felt thick and heavy. No one truly wanted to be here, but had found their lives turned upside down, or never starting out right from the beginning. I felt the impression that many were forced to come here, or chose this as their last effort to reach out. Did anyone truly believe that talking to a circle of strangers would solve their problems? They would still be there when they woke up.

Maybe it was just solace in the fact that they weren't the only ones out there with serious issues. These group discussions always seemed pointless to me. It was like we were all ghosts in a graveyard, talking about how life had been, what went wrong and what we missed. But none of it mattered because we were all still dead.

"Starting from my left, young man, can you briefly introduce yourself?" Mr. Wells gestured towards a boy that looked no older than me. He had curly red hair, an acne ridden face, and large lips. He trembled when he spoke.

"My. My...name is Eric Flores. I'm...I'm twenty years old."
Silence drifted throughout the room. I pondered if it was from the shock

of Eric's voice sounding so squeaky and childlike, or merely that no one was paying attention.

"Ok, thank you Eric. Could you tell us a little bit more about yourself and what brings you in today?" Someone in the group coughed and then a few seconds later someone sneezed. Eric cleared his throat.

How fucking awkward was this all?

And painful. It was like back in elementary school where you were forced to speak up and introduce yourself to the class. I felt bad for Eric.

"I'm from Brooklyn...I ma moved there from Florida five years ago. I...I go to Brooklyn Community College. I...I mean I went to Brooklyn Community College, but I dropped out."

"And why did you drop out, Eric?" Mr. Wells asked him gently.

"My...my doctor told my parents it was...was what would be best for my health."

Eric was bullied when he moved to New York, I thought. Most likely before that as well. For his looks, or his voice, or maybe his tiny, timid frame. Easy target. Eric probably never had a job and still lived with his parents. Never had a girlfriend or went on a date. He couldn't stay motivated enough to finish school and was probably seeing a psychiatrist. Eric most likely tried self harm numerous times and his parents were forcing him to seek additional help. Eric felt invisible, yet hyper-visible to evil people. Eric sounded unwanted, and alone in the world. Eric sounded very familiar.

What a loser.

Molly's voice painfully pierced my skull. I felt a headache coming on as my temples began to throb. Eric began to speak again.

"I'm here because...because..."

The entrance door slammed shut suddenly, startling us all. My head shot up from the floor. Everyone but me turned to look as a pair of athletic feet began running towards the group. The feeling of familiar dread washed over me as the person came closer. It couldn't be...

"Sorry, I'm late," a male voice shouted. Closer and closer he sprinted towards the group. "The traffic got me. An accident happened ahead and then I had to make a detour."

No...it couldn't be...

"Happy to be here and meet you all!" the man said, as he came closer.

No...it couldn't be. But the aura that filled the room told me otherwise.

"Hello!" Mr. Wells greeted the man. "Glad you could make it. We were just getting started. Ladies and gentlemen, another volunteer tonight!"

It was him. Again. He found me.

Uh oh, Jayd. Hehehehe
"I'd like you all to meet Paul McPhearson.

Just as his name was said, he came into view. Mr. Wells had pulled up a chair between himself and Eric. With one swift movement, the man leaped over the chair and sat down. He flashed a smile and ran his eyes amongst the circle.

I quickly dug my chin into my sweater, hoping he hadn't noticed me. I had a hoodie on my sweater and it was over my head. I hoped it concealed my face.

What type of karmic shitty luck did I have? Life wasn't finished playing its joke on me and had to continue to take digs after digs. It wouldn't give up. Tortured and berated. I was destined for both, wasn't I? It was bad enough...and it had just got a whole lot worse. To say the walls were inching closer in, and the ceiling was slowly crashing down was to say the least. I was stuck in a cycle of eternal punishment.

Mr. Wells continued.

"Paul contacted me directly to take the place of a former volunteer who tragically is not here with us today. I admire him for that. For those of you that haven't been made aware, a past volunteer by the name of Melanie Medela, died tragically earlier this year. Melanie was a treasure to this program, and always helped out when in need. I'm sure those of you who attended when she was present can agree to that."

Murmurs of agreement and head nods came from many in the room.

"Melanie always was eager to assist us here at Mental Health Matters, and she will be greatly missed. Condolences to you Paul." Mr. Wells ended with one hand on his chest and another on Paul's back.

"Thank you, Mr. Wells, and a good afternoon to you all! I'm glad to be here. And thank you Mr. Wells, on the kind words about my late fiancé. Melanie's loss is a loss not only to me, but to us all. Although she is not here in the flesh, she is here in spirit and she would want me to be here, supporting you all. Melanie was an advocate for mental health. She wanted to become an emergency room physician, and hoped to save those who had tried to take their own lives."

Haziness flooded my view and his talking became more and more unclear as I zoned out. My stomach and throat tightened and I felt as though I would slip out of my seat at any moment. Lines of water raced down my back. My hands and feet were cold, despite the warmth of the room. I had to force myself to zoom out. I couldn't listen to him anymore. Oh why, why, why?

Because you deserve it, Jayd. And now you can no longer run from it.

Paul McPhearson, the tall, handsome, fiancé of the late Melanie Medela was sitting across from me. The man I had tried tirelessly to avoid across New York had once again found his way to me. Had he been stalking me? Or following me undercover? Or was this just an unlucky fate that we kept running into each other out of the millions of people in New York?

His handsome face was etched in my mind the moment I saw him on the news in a photo beside Melanie. Underneath the photo, he was described as the loving and doting fiancé and that they were soon to be married before the tragic accident. His chiseled jaw, short beard and honey eyes were perfectly symmetrical on his face. If you saw him once, you would never forget that face. He looked like the men you'd see in a high end men's magazine. Good looking, well put together, mysterious, and successful.

Now he had an audience, and there was no doubt that once he recognized me, he would stand up and let it be known that I was the very girl that caused the death of his fiancé. And then I would rightfully be berated and humiliated and booed out of the building.

It took me a moment to realize dozens of eyes were on me, including his.

Darting from left to right while avoiding directly looking at anyone, I focused on Mr. Wells.

"...Yes?" I said, hesitantly, asking him what I already knew.

"It's your turn, Miss!" Mr. Wells said gently. "Please, introduce yourself to us all."

"Oh..s-sorry!" I stammered, not realizing initially, that I had zoned out for a while. "My name is Ashley Duncan. I'm from Harlem, New York. I'm nineteen years old and I work at an antique store and I am not in college yet. I'm here...for support."

The name slipped out of my mouth so seamlessly, I hadn't noticed at first that it was completely made up. His presence disrupted things and I had to stay unknown now. Miraculously, Paul had not recognized me. What a pity. A part of me wanted everyone here to know me and what had happened. To know Jayd Broussard and maybe not judge her. After all, everyone here had problems and addiction and pasts.

"Thank you, Ashley!" Mr. Wells said. "Welcome!"

By the next hour we had gotten through introducing ourselves or reintroducing ourselves and were then broken up into groups of four. Debra picked out the groups and Paul was given pieces of paper and a pencil to pass around. The only names of all the people here that I remembered were Eric, Candie, and the old woman who I noticed earlier whose name was Rose. This was the typical breakout session I had dealt with all my life. And as usual I would remain mostly silent and observe.

I was put in a group with Rose, and two other men. One of the men looked like a burly lumberjack, with dark hair and eyes. I think his name was Tom. The other man had a medium build, dark blonde, hair and green eyes. There was a long cut on his face, lining the edge of his jaw to his left ear. I wonder how he got it. Our group was silent as Mr. Wells announced the process of our session.

When Paul reached our group with the pencils and paper, I hesitantly reached for both as he stood behind me passing them out. He smelled newly fresh and clean. He must have gone for a morning jog and went home to freshen up before coming here. He greeted us all.

"Hi everyone! Thanks for coming," he said to our group. "Here you go!"

Thank god he didn't notice me. Before I knew it the scent drifted away as he moved on to give the next group their supplies. Mr. Wells spoke up.

"Now I would like all of you to take a piece of paper and a pencil, and write the very thing, the very reason you are here– and what led up to that reason. You will be sharing this with the room."

And there it was. I would be found out after all. My throat clenched, and my eyes darted towards the exit.

"For those of you who do not wish to share, don't worry. Everyone will be leaving their names off of their notes. You won't be reading your own statement. We will be passing each paper around to another group, and they will read out what you have written. You all will remain anonymous."

The air in the room was still stale. I paused to listen. I think I could hear the pitter patter of rain outside.

"Now, please begin. Share as much or as little as you feel, although, I would encourage you all to share your deepest inner thoughts and trauma. We are all connected, and it doesn't matter who reads your note as it could be that same person going through your same pain. So, let us start, we have ten minutes and then we will switch messages and read them out loud."

The sound of scribbling erupted from around the room. I stared down at my paper with my pencil in my hand.

But wouldn't he still figure out who I was? If I told them why I was really here and that I had tried to take my life and ended up taking another, wouldn't that let Paul know that I was here? That the killer of his fiancé was in the same room?

Duh.

I jumped in pain as Molly pinched my arm, then spirited across the room, tapping on everyone's head as she went from group to group. I watched her carefully as she went around to every group and then spirited towards the front entrance. She turned around to look at me, and then eagerly began to beckon me to leave with her.

My eyes shifted to the clock up on the wall above the restroom doors. Five minutes down. Five more to go. I glanced back at my blank sheet of paper and down at my pencil. Like with the weight of a brick on it, I lifted my arm with my pencil in hand and moved it towards the paper. I began scribbling.

"I was bullied in school and out of it. I'm shy and I have no friends. I feel everything. The good and the bad. It doesn't help either way. When I feel bad, I just want to roll up and die, and when I feel good, I want to die even more because I know I'll never have that consistently in my life. I am alone. My mother says I am unique. She says that because she is my mother. I know that I am a freak. A loser. A stain on the Earth amongst the endless clean spaces. I'm here because I'm tired of feeling. Isn't that sad? Who gets tired of feeling? Feeling is a part of being human. Maybe I'm not human. I'm here because I'm crazy, pathetic, and I need help. But I know that I can never get that help. Because I don't deserve it. I'm here but I know I shouldn't be here."

And with that, I stood up, grabbed my things and raced to the exit, leaving my group and my note behind on my chair.

Chapter 18

Am I selfish?

They had decided to keep my identity private, despite me being an adult, as respect due to the circumstances of my...accident.

Those closest to Mama knew, however, mostly because Aunt Opal told them. Our entire building knew. Their eyes pierced through me as I went in and out of our apartment building. I could try to ignore them but I felt their curiosity and disdain. I heard the gossip that floated in the air even after it had been spoken. I sensed their auras change, their hearts skip a beat, and their emotions waver whenever I was around.

Sylvia told me to leave work early today. I was sulking too much and ruining her mood.

An empty bottle of vodka lay beside me, halfway hidden under the bed. I had been at Pat's earlier before he kicked me out and told me to go home and lay down before I suffered alcohol poisoning. He tried to take my vodka bottle, but I ran out before he could.

Mama and Aunt Opal were watching TV in the living room and Norman lay beside me on the bed, deep in slumber. The lights are off in my room and the window is shut. A throbbing pain emits from my temples and the back of my eyeballs. It feels as though my brain is trying to break out of my skull. Was it the throbbing pain of guilt? In the back of my mind, I thought about her every day. Flashes of her face. His face. Their faces. Like the flash of a camera their images emerged and then faded.

She died in the midst of panic. Flashing around and attempting to grab hold of anything. I was barely conscious but I remember her face and when I looked up, I remembered his face and their faces. The look of absolute terror and fear.

I remember it as if it had happened only a few minutes ago.

We flew in the air, plunging into the water with her arms wrapped around my waist, squeezing me like a too-tight corset. Her grip on my waist was iron clad and when we hit the water it felt as though I had hit the pavement. It knocked me backwards, and a sharp pain shot up from my knees to my head. I didn't know who she was at the time, but I knew that someone behind me had shouted and grabbed a hold of me. In the water, I knew someone was there with me.

While still grabbing me by the waist, she was kicking upwards and pivoting her arms and body to stay afloat. We were rapidly sinking. I was drifting in and out of consciousness at this point and she was shouting at the people above to get help. A woman's voice was shouting. Some please, get help. Help us.

It was only minutes, but it felt like hours. I knew I was going to die and had already accepted my fate. It had horrifyingly then occurred to me that someone else was also now going to die because of me. I'm sorry, whoever you are. I'm so sorry.

I looked up and saw the tiny outline of people, and a handsome face of a man being pulled back by a group of people. It looked like he was prepared to jump over as well. It must be her loved one. Oh, fuck. I'm so sorry. Dozens of people lined the bridge, looking down in horror, shouting, waving their arms.

With all of her might, she paddled and paddled. My back hit something hard. I would later learn that it was one of the pile caps on one of the bridge's piers. With all of her lasting strength she pulled my weight up and on top of the cap. It wasn't enough room for the two of us and the water was rough that day. I had purposely picked a stormy day to die, reflective of my inner turmoil. She held me against the pier. Her breathing was heavy and weak.

You're okay, sweetie. You're going to be okay, she had said.

No. No. Please lady, save yourself. I'm not worth it. What are you doing? Save yourself!

It would take a half an hour before someone got to us. By that time, she had lost her strength holding my worthless body up on the cap as it threatened to fall over. The beating down of the rain and the rough current was too much for her. I saw her sink down below as I was pulled into a boat above. I saw the panic on her face as she came to a realization that she wasn't going to make it. The only one of us would. I wondered if she now regretted saving me.

She was pulled under and away by the current, thrashing and flailing, but too tired to keep going. Water was filling her lungs and she was choking. In the last seconds of her life, I saw her fade away. The life on her face had completely faded away. And in that split second, she looked at peace. She looked at me with eyes that showed that she accepted her fate. With her arms outstretched above her body, she sank further and was pulled farther away until she could no longer be spotted.

I was now in a rescue boat and the screams and shouts could be heard over the thundering storm above. I was pulled this way and that way. I was now almost completely unconscious. I felt the heavy pressure of someone's hands on my chest, performing CPR.

Why bother? I had thought. Just toss me back into the water.

There was another one!

Oh god! She went under! We need backup!

Someone get medical on this one! We need a diver!

She's gone! I don't see her. The current's too strong! She's gone!

What have I done? She's gone. Because of me. It wasn't worth it, lady. Why did you do it?
Just throw me back in.

And then it all went black.

It would take two days for search and recovery efforts to find her body.

I woke up a few months later never before wishing that I had taken Melanie's place that day.

Reaching my arms down, I gulped down the rest of my vodka through my tears. My head was pounding harder than ever.

Good. Maybe it'll pound so hard it'll break out of my skull and I'll suffer a horrible death. Maybe then all would be forgiven, I thought to myself.

In the corner of my room, Molly was up against the wall, arms crossed, and smirking.

Chapter 19

Sawdust particles filled my nose. Sylvia was doing some construction upstairs and some workers had come in earlier today.

"Atchoo!" I sneezed then blinked rapidly a few times. I had been working for her for about two months now, and a lot of progress had been made with unpacking, cleaning, dusting, and organizing the antiques. I quickly looked around the small room and a feeling of calm and elation washed over me. I was very fond of this little place, and liked being here alone when Sylvia was out. In my free time, I would zero in on an antique and tell its story. How old it was and where it came from. Who owned it and how it ended up here. Summer was coming to an end very soon, and it was getting chiller. The antique shop gave me a warm and cozy feeling, perfect for the upcoming fall and winter.

Sylvia had left an hour ago to run some errands. I was working today for some overtime. Today was unbearable, though, with the smell of sawdust in the air. Thank goodness my shift was almost over.

Across from the cashier desk where I sat, there was a small shelf with a row of used candles. Beside the candles was a small lighter. I spotted the shelf weeks earlier and always wanted to see what scents they were.

Moving from around the large cashier's desk, I went over to the shelf and picked up a candle.

"Vanilla and Lavender" I read the scent on the jar aloud. I picked up another one.

"Milk and Honey", was written in italics on the paper cover. Another candle read, "Ocean Breeze", "Twilight", and "Bunch of Flowers". Sniffing each one, I liked "Twilight" the best. It smelled like some ethereal, otherworldly, fairy. Lighting the candle with the small lighter, I returned to the cashier desk and sat the candle on the corner of the desk, far out of anyone's way.

My eyes drifted to the tiny lit flame. An aroma that I couldn't describe in words filled my nostrils and the sawdust scent began to diminish. The flame of the fire was calming as I watched it dance rapidly in the air. My eyelids began to get heavy and I felt like I was about to drift off. I was so mesmerized by the flame that I didn't even hear the door open or see him come in.

He stood with his hands on the tip of the cashier's desk. Seeing the hands, I immediately stood up.

Paul was dressed in a black sweatsuit and some sneakers. On his right wrist was an expensive looking watch, and on his left ring finger, what appeared to be an engagement ring.
My heart sank into my stomach as I noticed it. I quickly looked up at him and into his face. A pair of honey eyes and white teeth stood smiling back.

"What a charming little shop. It was hard as hell to find it, though!' he exclaimed. I stared at him.

Find? Was he looking for this shop?

"Sorry?" I said to him, "You were looking for this shop?"

"Well, I remember you said you worked at an antique shop at the group session the other day. There are hundreds of them in New York. Made a lot of calls, but I finally located you. You left early and I never got to ask you about your job. How are you, Ashley?"

I continued to stand and stare at him. What was he saying? He was looking for me? And who's Ashley? A sharp pain erupted from my tongue when I bit down on it, as I remembered that Ashley was the fake name I had given myself that day during the session.

"Uh, yeah! This is where I work," I stuttered, hoping he didn't notice or see the panic in my eyes or hear it in my voice. "I forgot I had an errand to run that day. I got a call from a relative. Sorry I had to leave early."

His perfectly symmetrical face and broad shoulders leaned further towards me. A look of sympathy crossed his face.

"It's no problem at all. I knew something probably had to have come up. It's a shame you missed the other activities, though. And your note you left on your seat before you took off." He gave me a small smile. "Every note was read aloud anonymously and from another individual. I really hope you weren't afraid or traumatized by the thought of that. The exercise was meant to acknowledge that problems know no color, gender, religion, or sexuality. We all go through things.

I slowly sat back down in the chair behind the cashier's desk. The man in front of me, the fiancé of the woman I murdered, was sympathetically conversing with me. Was smiling at me. Was being kind to me. I couldn't believe it.

"No!" I said. "It wasn't that at all. Really, I just had to run and get some things done."

"Then I hope you'll be back for our next session this upcoming weekend!" Paul said enthusiastically. "They'll try to implement more fun ideas and supportive measures for everyone. After all, the program is meant to help you heal."

No. I definitely won't. No offense to you, though.

Paul was very attractive and had a friendly aura. I could see why Melanie, or any woman would be drawn to him. He spoke and listened. I wondered if my silence was from the fear of possibly implicating my true identity, or from the overwhelming feeling that the room was slowly closing in again the second I spotted the engagement ring. A sharp pain in the back of my head began.

I'm so sorry Melanie. I could say it a million times, but it would never be enough.

"Ashley?" Paul said, his voice now taking on a more serious tone. I stood up again and our eyes met.

"As you may have heard at the beginning of the session, I lost my fiancé a few months ago, and it hasn't been easy for me at all. Whatever you're going through, just please know that you're not alone. Many people are suffering from something, and we often think that we're alone in that suffering and that it'll never end. Just please know that there is help out there."

I watched as he took a small note out of his sweat suit pocket and gently etched forward and laid it into my hand.

"If you decide not to come to a group session again, please just keep in touch. Reach out if you ever need anyone to talk to, Ashley. I know what it's like."

And with that, he gave one last smile before quickly disappearing out of the door, just as suddenly as he had come in. I had been looking down at the note before I noticed he was even gone.

On the note, scribbled in black ink was the name Paul McPhearson and a phone number below his name. Below this were a few words. *We all* deserve a place in this world. *I'd like to know more about your story.*

Peering intently at the paper, I could see the faint lines of writing on the back of the note.

Turning the note around and skimming the words on the back, I paused. It was the exact note I had left on my chair during the group session.

My cell phone rang and the sound of it startled me. I looked at the caller ID and the name Sylvia popped up.

"Make sure you lock up everything before I get back!" she said into the phone when I answered. "Last time you left the back door open! And goodnight. See you tomorrow!"

She hung up the phone and I just stood there, wondering what the fuck had just happened a few minutes ago and had I bitten off more than I could chew.

Chapter 20

"Get out of here, Mack!" Pat yelled. "I told you, I'm not buying that shit from you no more! It fucked me up last time!"

"Oh c'mon!" Mack yelled back. "How do you know it was my stuff? You be buying from all over!"

"Just get out!" Pat yelled. "And don't let me see your ugly face around here anymore!"

Mack cursed under his breath and whorled around, marching towards the door. I watched from the couch as the argument went down. Mack picked up his suitcase filled with his homemade drugs near the front entrance and was about to storm out before he noticed me way in the back.

"Hey you, little girl!" he shouted over at me. "Looking for something to turn you up tonight? I got everything from pills, to coke, to weed. Even gotta homemade elixir I made with some shrooms!"

The thundering footsteps of Pat came bursting from around the counter and in a millisecond, he was in Mack's face.

"I told you to get the fuck out of here Mack! He snarled as he had Mack by the collar. "Don't talk to her. Don't talk to me. Just get out! Don't come near her. I better not see you around here ever again!"

And with that, Pat shoved Mack out the door and slammed it shut. He angrily cursed under his breath as he headed back behind the bar counter and began rinsing glasses. I had never seen Pat that angry before. It was scary.

"And you! Little missy back there!" he turned to shout at me. "Get the hell up and go home! Sick of you lying around and getting drunk and passing out here. Go home and do that!"

"Fuck you, Pat!" I told him.

I scooted from the middle of the couch onto the end and put my head on the couch arm and gave a deep sigh. Pat would have to call the cops to get me out, and since he would never allow a cop in his bar, he'd have to drag me out himself. I wasn't going home for a while.

The bar was silent and the heavy sound of my breathing was all that could be heard. My eyes were shut because the lights made them hurt. I was having the worst headache of my life, and my stomach was threatening to empty its contents at any moment. I could feel a pair of eyes on me and tilted my head in Pat's direction.

"What?" I said. "What are you looking at?"

"What the hell is wrong with you?" he asked with a tone of disbelief. "You come in here and flop down and drink all day without saying a word. I know you have serious issues, but please, this is my place, Jayd. Have a little respect. Whatever you're going through you know I'm here to listen, but don't you ever swear at me like that in my own bar."

Another deep sigh escaped from my lips. Pat was the second most favorite person in my life, after Mama, so having him upset with me caused me to feel ashamed.

"I'm sorry, Pat." I told him. "I had an argument with my aunt today and really don't want to be at home right now."

An argument was an understatement. The neighbors on the floors above and below us could be heard protesting to my aunt and my shouting.

I had ended up deciding to go back to the group sessions for Mental Health Matters. Why? I didn't really know why. Had Paul convinced me to give it another shot, or did I simply feel bad for leaving too soon. There was an incompleteness that had been harvesting in me for a while, and between drinking, therapists, and sleeping, it was only mildly being addressed. Molly was becoming more annoying and crueler to me, and my depression seemed to be worsening. Did a part of me think Mental Health Matters could really be the thing that helped? Tracing Melanie's every step seemed to only remind me how much she was loved and what I took from the world.

I had just finished eating breakfast and Mama was humming in the kitchen. I would head over to the group session, and then meet with Janelle later. Mama made banana pancakes and turkey bacon, which I had devoured quickly. I was up and ready to head out right when Aunt Opal came slithering in. Aunt Opal was back from her vacation, much to my dismay. I knew that she lived here, but there was that massive hope in me that she would permanently move out and never come back. Maybe she could go live with Aunt Pearl and leave Mama and me alone. I felt great disappointment every time I saw that she returned.

"Well good morning to you!" she said to me as she ushered herself into the kitchen and went straight to the coffee pot. Mama already made coffee and I watched as Aunt Opal took out a mug and poured herself a cup. She was wearing a white and blue nightgown with a matching head scarf.

Norman walked in after her and went straight under the table and to my feet, begging for some food. He rubbed up against my leg and I bent down to stroke his head, completely ignoring Aunt Opal.

The sound of a cabinet door slamming shut startled me, and I looked up. Aunt Opal peered over at me with a frown on her face. Mama paused from washing a dish and tilted her head over, zeroing in on the impending conflict.

Not today, Aunt Opal. Leave me alone, bitch.

"I said good morning, Jayd!" she barked. "Did you not hear me?"

I quickly got up from the table and headed for the pantry to retrieve Norman some food.

"Good morning, Aunt Opal" I kept my head down and my back to her as I opened a can of cat food and poured it into Norman's bowl. He trotted over happily and began gulping it up.
I wanted to eagerly get out of Aunt Opal's presence and make my way to the group session, so I gave Mama a peck on the cheek and sprinted towards the door.

"Hold up!" a bellowing voice yelled out, stopping me just before I reached the door. "Where are you off to so early this morning?"

"I have a group session this morning to get to," I replied and reached for the door knob.

"What group session?" Aunt Opal asked. "Aren't you supposed to see your therapist today?"

"Yes," I said. "I'm going to see her afterwards."

"Yes, ma'am, Jayd. You say yes ma'am to me."

With my back still turned, I heard her walk towards the kitchen table and sit down.

"And where's the money you're supposed to be giving me this week towards your hospital bills?" I could hear Aunt Opal taking a sip from her mug before continuing. "Where's your application for school you were supposed to fill out?"

"Leave me alone…" I mumbled. I turned the knob to the kitchen door and pushed it open.

"Excuse me!" Aunt Opal shouted. "What did you say? Little girl, I'm tired of you fresh ass mouth!"

Hehehehehe

"Opal...please" Mama began. With my back still to them both, I felt her turn around and look in my direction. "Not today, Jayd. Please"

Hehehehehe

Molly was somewhere in the room, but I couldn't see her. She was laughing and mocking me more and more each and every day. It was beginning to get hard to ignore.

"You need to teach your daughter some manners and to stop sass mouthing me or I'll…"

"Or, you'll what?" I yelled. "Why can't you just leave!? Get the hell out and stay away! Go live with one of your little boyfriends and leave Mama and me alone! Just leave!"

A stunned silence entered the room and it stayed there as both my mother and my aunt looked at me, both shocked at what I had said. I meant every word of it. Aunt Opal flew from around the table and stopped a few feet from me. Her eyes were blazing with anger and her body shook. She looked like an angry crow.

"You...you.rotten little bit-"

"Opal," Mama shouted, stopping her. She ran between us and stretched out her arms. "Stop it! The two of you!"

"You crazy little bitch!" Aunt Opal shouted her words at me as if she were throwing knives. "Your mother is the one who can't stand you! You're the reason she has to work so hard!"

"Fuck you!" I shouted back at her. "My mother loves me! And I hate you! From the bottom of my heart and to the very core, I hate your very being and wish we weren't related!"

"Jayd?!" Mama looked at me with such shock and hurt in her eyes and voice. Aunt Opal shook uncontrollably.

"Every single time I'm near, you have something to say to me. Just leave me alone! Don't say anything to me!" I was shaking now too and tears began to stream down my face, as I yelled at her. "Act like I'm not here and I'll act like you aren't!"

"I wish you weren't here!" Aunt Opal shouted. "You're a nutcase. You caused someone to die and you have the gall to say I should leave? You shouldn't even be here! You're a selfish, lazy, little cow, and you put us all in debt due to your actions! I bet that woman sure wished you weren't here and she was!"

Oops. Hehehehe

"OPAL! How dare you?!" Mama shrieked.

Her voice was so loud I thought the windows would blow out. I stood staring at her in disbelief and a tiny smirk appeared on her lips. Silence, even more quiet than death itself floated throughout the room. She had paralyzed me with her words and she knew it. She had conjured up the worst thing she could possibly say to me. She had spit out my biggest fear and guilt since the day I woke up and was informed on what happened. On what I did. The dreaded realization I had come to know since I awoke from my coma. The very thing that tore me up inside, depressed me, and agonized me to no possible end. Aunt Opal had called me a murderer without actually calling me one.

So, I stood staring into her angry, glowering eyes until I couldn't stand there anymore. Quietly, I turned around and walked out of the kitchen and back to my room.

I wouldn't be going to the group session today. I no longer felt like it. I felt drained, embarrassed, and defeated at the same time. I felt as though I had been stabbed in the stomach and was still reeling from the shock, high on adrenaline. Mama called out to me but I ignored her. I couldn't think or respond. My arms and legs moved as if they had a mind of their own.

"Jayd!" Mama called out. "Come, here baby!"

"Let her go, Ruby!" Aunt Opal said.

"Shut up, Opal! Don't you ever talk to her again!" Mama shouted.

I left the apartment in a hurry and slammed the door shut, not daring to look back. I was on the edge of exploding and my mind was scattered as a million things went through them. I couldn't stay in the apartment right now, so I headed to my second sanctuary. Neighbors stuck their heads out of their doors to look where the noise had come from and I flew past them towards the exit. Not bothering to take the elevator, I ran down the stairwell and out of the building to Pat's. I couldn't tell whether I was more sad or angry. I still can't tell even now as I laid back and downed another bottle.

I lifted my head up to glance over at Pat. He looked back at me with both defiance and concern. We looked at each other for a few moments before his face softened.

"You're welcome here whenever you like, but please, let me know what's going on with you."

And with that, I was back in Pat's good graces.

Pat had the bar door open, as he had been sweeping the bar out earlier. I eyed something coming from that direction and turned to look. Standing directly in the front doorway was Molly. Through my inebriated vision her silhouette went in and out of view. I forced myself to focus on her and my heart skipped a beat when I saw how angrily she was glaring at me. Molly was beginning to scare me. She shoved me on my way here to Pat's, and scratched me a few times when I sat down on the couch. Hurtful words were common with Molly, but physical violence was rare. Thank goodness she couldn't come into the bar. She looked like she wanted to rip my head off right now.

As I watched her glare at me with an unprovoked anger, I thought of Janelle.

I need to go see her today. We needed to talk. Urgently.

Oh, and I should probably stop drinking.

Chapter 21

"So... he stopped by a few days ago..."

"Hmmm?", Janelle said softly as she lifted her head from the files she was rummaging through in a cabinet beside her desk. She had her back turned away from me. The large window behind her was wide open and a mildly chilly breeze fluttered the curtains. Below I could hear the traffic of New York and the bustling of people.

"Paul", I said to her. "Paul McPhearson is his name. He came by a few days ago to talk to me."

Janelle gave me a quizzical look and then turned back around to fish out a few more files before shutting and locking the cabinet. She placed the files on her desk and clapped her hands in triumph.

"That should be all of them!" She then turned to me and smiled. "Now Jayd, what were you saying? Who's Paul McPhearson?"

"He's Melanie's fiancé!" I blurted out. "Or, at least he was Melanie's fiancé. I first started seeing him around and then he came to a group session that Melanie used to volunteer at. Later, he came to my job!"

The nervousness in my voice could be felt to the very core. Janelle studied my expression and eyed me closely, peering at me intently. Her eyes widened after a moment when she saw what I was alluding to.

"Oh, I see." she finally said. "Did he recognize you?"

"No!" I told her. "At least I don't think he did. He didn't give an indication that he knew who I was. I told him my name was Ashley Duncan."

Janelle looked at me in slight surprise before an awkward, tight-lipped smile crossed her lips.

"Jayd...really?" she began.

"I don't want him to know who I am!" The nervousness had now switched to a tone of fear. But not just any fear. It was a deep-seated urgent fear of avoiding what could be one of the worst revelations of my actions. It was heartbreaking to know that Melanie's close friends despised the girl that caused her death, but if the love of her life found out who I was, it would be a complete disaster.

A sudden movement behind Janelle caught my eye and I glanced behind her at the window. The curtains fluttered gently back and forth in the wind as a creeping dread began to fill me. She appeared in the blink of an eye, sitting on the window sill. Her legs were crossed and her body was turned in my direction. The curtains masked her face and upper body. I could barely make out Molly's expression but something in me knew that it wasn't pleasant.

"Jayd, please. I want you to listen." Janelle had stood up and made her way around her desk. She parked herself right in front of her desk and half sat on it, thankfully blocking Molly out of my view. With both hands resting at her sides, she looked me directly in the eye.

"Jayd, I know you're not a very confrontational person, I can sense that from you. You appear passive and shy."

"But after getting to analyze you a bit more and talking and listening to you, I get that that isn't what you truly are." Janelle continued. "I see a girl trapped in the memory of her traumatic past, unable to move on and forgive herself. Unable to find peace and get closure."

"You're punishing yourself, Jayd. For something you had no idea would happen. You were suffering and wanted to be put out of your misery. You are just as much a victim as she was. Remember that. Always. You cannot turn back time and you cannot wish away the pain if you never address the root cause of it. You cannot change people's opinions of you and what happened, and you shouldn't have to. For the love of god Jayd, I want and need you to be kinder to yourself and be patient with yourself."

As I listened to her, I let her words seep into my brain. She had such a comforting and supportive voice.

But I knew that what she was saying was all in vain. At the end of the day, I caused Melanie to die. My selfish action of trying to take my life caused her death. In a cruel twist of fate, death took Melanie and not me.

"Talk to him," Janelle said. "I would let Paul know who I was. You might not believe this Jayd, but you owe him that at least. To know who you are."

"What if he gets upset with me? Shouts or tries to harm me?"

"That's just the risk you're going to have to take Jayd. Meet him at a police station or somewhere else open, crowded, and safe. Explain to him and let him know that you sympathize with what he's feeling. But even more than that, let him know that you are a victim in this as well. That you cannot change what happened and that you understand if he is upset with you."

"Jayd, you need closure" Janelle said as she held my gaze. "You need an end to this horrible chapter in your life. If you decide to never face this head on, and keep running away torturing yourself, you will never heal."

I didn't know much about Paul, but I felt strongly that he was not the type of person to violently lash out. He seemed understanding and kind. But would he be the same if he knew my real identity?

"Ok," I lied to her. "I'll tell him." Janelle beamed at me.

"Great!" she said, as she got up and moved back around her desk to sit down. "This will be good for you, Jayd. For both you and Paul."

Behind Janelle I could see that the window sill was now empty. Molly was gone, but I heard her voice echo in head.

She doesn't know what she's talking about, Jayd. The familiar demonic voice in my head said.
Paul will hate you like everybody hates you. And when he finds out, you'll be through. You shouldn't be here, and you know that. Janelle even knows that. She's just telling you what you want to hear. It's time you face the facts. You are a M-U-R-D-E-R-E-R.

As a single tear gathered in my eye, I let it fall and drip off my chin. Janelle was humming a sweet tune now. The sound of static began to ring out of my ears as I tuned the world out. The world that was the only hell that I knew. That seeped in every corner and dripped off of every crevice. It was a reminder that I was trapped in this forever.

Chapter 22

"That's all you're going to eat?" Mama asked me as she bent over and peered at my half-eaten plate of pancakes. A slight hurt could be heard in her voice.

"Yeah, I'm not too hungry this morning," I told her, placing my fork beside the pancakes and gulping down the rest of my orange juice.

Aunt Opal was gone again. Apparently, she was off to visit a few friends in another state or something. I suspected that was a lie the moment Mama told me, and knew Mama probably had something to do with Opal being gone.

Today I would be biking to Central Park and then around and through the park for a while. It was Sunday morning and the weather was perfect. Apparently, Melanie, in addition to being an avid yoga and jogger, loved to bike around New York City. I was dressed in a long sleeve tee-shirt and yoga pants with some running shoes on. Mama was still in her nightgown.

"Well, okay," Mama said gently. "If you aren't feeling well, let me know."

"I feel fine Mama," I leaned forward and gave her a hug. She strongly embraced me back and held on to me, planting a huge kiss on my forehead. She was taller than, but only slightly. I would soon pass her in height, she recently told me.

Today the apartment building was noisier than usual. Being that it was Sunday, many of the tenants were getting ready for church or going out to brunch later. Our family doesn't go to church anymore. We stopped when I got to middle school. Mama had fallen out with a pastor on some of her opinions and his constant flirting, and Aunt Opal never came along with us anyway. I was always awkward in church, couldn't sing so I wasn't in the choir and unlike many of the other kids, I constantly asked the pastor questions about the Bible. These days Mama considers herself a spiritualist. Whatever that means. I honestly didn't know what I believed in.

With breakfast done, I gathered my things and headed towards the door, bending down to rub Norman before I left.

Outside I unlocked my bike that I had rented the day and headed towards Central Park. Staying inside of the bike lanes, I avoided distracted people that had stopped directly in the bike lane and weaved in and out of traffic. Ten minutes later I was slowing down, completely out of breath. I knew I was getting out of shape, but this was just sad, I thought to myself. The constant drinking wasn't doing me any favors.

Taking in deep breaths, I stopped and looked around. As usual, New York was busy, full of lively people and uptightness. The streets teamed with the hopeful, the wannabe famous, the gentrifiers, the broken, the chic, the rich, the poor, and the invisibles. The air stunk of ruthless ambition, exploitation, desperation, and piss. Good old New York. I didn't know any other place to call home but it.

I rode on, focusing on my breathing and getting to the park safely. In a little over an hour, I reached Central Park and was instantly met with an abundance of dogs being walked, little kids running around, and food carts. Stopping right at the entrance, I took a sip of water from a large water bottle Mama brought me.

The plan for today would be biking around the park and just enjoying the day, something I almost never did. This evening I would be working at Sylvia's and then later, Mama and I would go out to eat. Her treat.

I rode through the front entrance and began to slowly peddle down the path. On either side of me benches of people sat and people walked their dogs and jogged in all directions. Flowers and trees were in their late stages, slowly dwindling as Fall approaches.

As I rode, my eyes darted around, checking my surroundings. The waterfall of emotions that passed through me were unbearable, and they were not my own. I felt frustrated, then excited, then pessimistic, bored, and content at the same time. The girl walking past with her dog, the little kids playing on the grass, the man smoking in the corner, the little boy being scolded by his mom far to my left and the woman sitting down reading a book on the bench. All of them. It was like I could feel everything they felt.

It was like this. Always.

I felt them more than I felt myself. I almost could never tell what I was really feeling or if they were my emotions at all. This made for a shitty childhood, because it was like everything affected me without me wanting it to. I often misidentified what I was feeling, and my emotions never made sense. When I should have been happy, I felt depressed. When I was depressed, people became annoyed, because I should have been glad. Mama often said that I was just very intuitive. She told me that there was nothing wrong with me and that I was just sensitive. That I was just a very empathetic girl.

But to feel all the time, everyone and everything was like a curse. Life seemed to pass me by. I didn't even feel alive most times. Like I was dead…and awake at the same time.

"I'm seriously beginning to think you're stalking me."

I jumped from the sound of his voice. I had been so deep in thought, and peddling, I didn't notice him sitting on the bench a few feet away.

Paul was laying back on the bench with one arm stretched out and the other one in his lap. Dark honey eyes met mine and a smirk crossed his lips. I quickly analyzed him. He had bags under his eyes and looked tired. Depleted. His smirk, although charming, had a deep sadness to it. He was sporting a black and green tracksuit and had what appeared to be an exquisite mountain bike that leaned on the back of the bench.

"Excuse me?", I said to him. "It's you who's been stalking me! You're conveniently everywhere I am, sir."

He smiled and chuckled again. A sorrowful chuckle. And then he looked down at his lap and then at the ground as if he was embarrassed.

"Perhaps it's just chance, eh?" Paul said. "How are you today, Ashley?"

"I'm fine. Just out for a little exercise." I hopped off my bike and leaned it against the opposite side of the bench where he sat. I wondered what he was thinking and why he looked so unhappy. From the time I met him, and kept bumping into him, he always appeared cheerful. It was I who was the one that walked around unhappy.

Maybe he was thinking about Melanie…

"I see," he said, nodding. "It's a nice day to do it as well."

I watched him carefully. Could this be my chance to tell him who I was? The park was crowded, so if he erupted in anger and tried something…

"Would you like to sit down?" he asked, tearing through my thoughts. A feeling of awkwardness and nervousness sprung like a weed in me. And guilt.

Did I deserve to be here and intrude on his grieving and remembrance of his fiancé? He kept talking as if he hadn't noticed that I didn't respond to him.

"Missed you yesterday at the group session. It was great and we all got to know each other a lot better."

Yesterday.

Yesterday was a nightmare. A very bad dream that met me when I walked into the kitchen this morning.

"I wasn't feeling too well, that's all" I said to him. He nodded in sympathy and then looked back downward at the ground. I watched him and looked at his eyes. He was very handsome, and I had spotted a few women eyeing him as they walked by. As I continued to watch him, I thought about disrupting him from his train of thought and dropping the bomb of my identity on him, but something told me not to. Something was telling me that this wasn't the right time.

His eyes began to look hazy. The lively honey colored eyes that they normally were seemed to darken more and more. He looked as if he were focusing on something intently right in front of him, but also daydreaming about something far away.

It was times like this that I wished I were truly invisible. I wished he never saw me riding in his direction. What could I possibly say to him? Why did I think that I could just go up to him and explain everything? As if it would be that easy?

I should just walk away. Why was I still standing here? What did I hope to accomplish? No, I can't do it. It could bring me closure, but would it bring him it? Oh, Melanie. I'm so sorry.

Silence drifted between us as I continued to watch him. He looked as if he was so far away. Like he was trapped in another world in a body that remained in reality. I knew the feeling.

Suddenly, he stood up.

"Do you want to go for a bike ride, Ashley?" Paul exclaimed, as his eyes and smile lit up. He had instantly transformed into the Paul I had seen so many times before. Like a light switch, he was back.

I didn't answer right away because I had been both startled and surprised by the change.

"Please," he said eagerly. "I'd like to take a ride. Maybe we can talk more. I feel like there might be an unnecessary wall between you and I."

I was too stunned to say anything and I watched as he unlocked his bike from the back of the bench and rolled it over to the path.

My mind was a whirlpool of questions. Why would he want to chat with me? What's with the sudden change in demeanor? Did he suspect something about me? Or did he just want to talk with another trauma filled person?

Paul had a light jacket tied around his waist which he took off and put on. He glanced over at me and my eyes fell to the ground as I thought of what to do. How would I escape this situation and what would I say to him? I felt him continue to look at me with that sympathetic look of his.

"I don't bite," he softly chuckled. "And besides, if you suspect me of anything you have my permission to carry my mace and use it on me." He unzipped one of his jacket pockets and pulled a small black container with a key chain on it. He extended his arm and handed it to me.

Cautiously, I took it out of his hand and then looked straight into his face.

"It's not that," I told him, putting the mace in my own jacket. "It's just that I'm not very fast. There's no way I could keep up with you."

Paul paused for a moment before his face lit up and laughter erupted from him.

"I'm not particularly fast myself, but thanks for the compliment." As he chuckled, I glanced at his athletic figure and knew he couldn't be telling the truth. He was built like a track star and I could see the abs and muscles threatening to rip from out of his shirt.

"My late finance was the athletic one. She enjoyed everything outdoorsy, and was the one who got me into fitness." He smiled again showing perfect white teeth.

"Anyway, we'll go slow as I'd like to chat and get to know you more." Paul walked from around his bike and extended a hand.

"Although you may already know, I'm Paul McPhearson, born and raised in Manhattan."

I took his hand and shook it hesitantly.

"I'm Ashley," I said. "Ashley Duncan."

"Well, Ashley. Now that we've fully introduced ourselves, shall we ride on?" He made an exaggerated gestures towards my bike and I nodded, giving him an awkward grin.

I put one leg around my bike and pushed off. And so, we rode around Central Park and chatted about nothing in particular. He laughed, I snickered. He would exaggerate and I would roll my eyes. Like old friends catching up, we rode on and talked for hours.

At one point, I passed Molly standing in the grass. She looked heartbroken.

Chapter 23

"No way? Really?"

"Born and raised," Paul replied. "I'm a Bronx boy through and through."

The waitress had just dropped off our drinks. I ordered a small vanilla chai latte. Paul ordered a cup of coffee, black with no sugar. In the background of chatter in the small cafe, classical music played. We were one of the few people here. Paul picked out the place, telling me it was a hidden little gem.

"That's cool. I'm from Harlem. Been there all my life."

Across the small table, Paul's smile reached his eyes. Today he was sporting a casual outfit, a tee-shirt, jeans, and boots. I had on my usual tee-shirt, jeans, and sneaker combo.

"Y know Ashley, I've been thinking of possibly moving back there. When I moved to Manhattan after graduate school, I never got used to the stuffy vibe. Melanie could handle it like a pro though."

Paul had invited me out today at a cafe. It was a couple of days after we met up at the park and I was surprised when he dropped by my job again and asked if I wanted to go out. I immediately told him no.

"I don't really do restaurants," I lied, food was life for me. "And I have to work all this morning."

"It's just a little cafe I've been wanting to go back to." He said. "It has the best coffee!"

It was early that morning and Sylvia had been scanning the shelves in the back when she walked up and saw me and Paul conversing.

"Go! Go!" she told me, ushering me out the door with her tiny frame. "You could use a break. You work overtime everyday now. Go relax" She looked over at Paul.

"Hello young man. Take her away please. You can come back in the evening and work!" Sylvia gave me a wink and before I could respond, she abruptly turned around and went towards the back of the shop and into the storage room.

I had no choice but to head out with Paul, and thirty minutes later here we were, sitting and chatting like old friends.

It almost made me forget about her…and who she was to him.

Because you're selfish, Jayd. Look at you! Chatting up with the man's whose fiancé you murdered! You're a coward. Tell him who you are!

Trying my best to push Molly out of my head, I focused on Paul's face. He had a gorgeous caramel complexion and a few small moles on his chin and neck. His hair was cut low and neat. I focused on his lips as he spoke.

"It's a great job. You meet a lot of intelligent and successful people. But I often thought that it wasn't for me, but rather what my mom wanted me to be."

He was talking about his career on Wall Street as a business analyst. Paul apparently came from a rough area of the Bronx before moving to

Manhattan for college and meeting Melanie. They met at a party and it was love at first sight.

I turned away a few times as Paul spoke about him and Melanie. They were truly in love and had so much going for themselves.

"Tell me, if you don't mind Paul, tell me more about Melanie. I'm curious. What was she like?" I forced myself to turn to him and ask. I knew I was entering risky territory by asking Paul this, and it almost seemed hypocritical. What if he wasn't ready to talk about Melanie to anyone? What if he, like I, was still deeply traumatized by losing the love of his life?

In the weeks that I had been trying to discover all that I could about Melanie, I felt that I had barely scratched the surface. Now here, right in front of me, was a person that could give me the information that I needed. But…was it the right thing to ask of him?

Before I could internally battle whether or not I should tell Paul to forget about what I asked, he let out a sigh and then in a completely dejected tone he started talking.

"She was my best friend," he began. He spoke almost as if it pained him. "Melanie was the one who encouraged me to get up every day and brace myself for anything the world threw at us. She was a light at the end of a tunnel for many. Always supporting me and everyone she loved."

So, Melanie really was an angel, I thought. An angel that I took away from so many. So, did that make me a demon?
"She never, even in their worst condition, looked down on or judged others. When we first met in undergrad, I was intimidated by her." He

smirked as he recounted the story.

"I was with a few of my frat brothers and Melanie was in her own sorority. At the party when we first met, our eyes locked immediately. She was stunning and very charming. While other girls waited for the guys to approach, she walked right up to me and asked me what my name was. Years later we'd joke about that and how it would be something to tell our kids."

I suddenly felt queasy.

Kids.

Melanie and Paul were going to have kids.

I wanted to get up and leave, but knew how rude it would look and possibly how hurt he would be. And maybe…he might get suspicious of me. I struggled to stay in my seat as he went on. Each word that fell out of him was unbearable. I wondered if he could see my hands tightening around my cup, turning red from the grip I had on it.

"Melanie wanted to be an emergency physician and volunteer in underserved communities. She grew up privileged. Both parents were lawyers. They pushed her to succeed like nothing else. Her mom loved me. Dad, not so much."

As he talked, reminisces of my earlier school days emerged.

I was known as the quiet girl. The weirdo and the freak. The loser with no friends who had a beautiful Mama she could never look like. Younger

Jayd always had her head in the clouds on a different planet. She was never on time nor paying attention. She disturbed both teachers and students alike. Younger Jayd showed no interest in sports, but had a keen interest in reading and on days when everyone was outside at recess, Jayd was in the library, hidden behind a stack of books.

Younger Jayd was as invisible as she was hyper-visible, especially to bullies and irritated teachers who wished to make an example of her. She felt everything intensely without meaning to, and would come off as awkward to anyone she tried to explain her feelings to. Younger Jayd was often confused, depressed, and lonely. Younger Jayd was among the walking dead. She was living–at least up to the standards a person was supposed to live a life, and she would be seen floating from here to there, silent. She was shy, timid, and passive. She was inquisitive, cautious, and curious. She wasn't a trouble maker, yet always found herself in trouble.

Cruel words could and did pull Jayd out of the company of her own mind, the one place where she thought she was safe. They cut into her like blades and traumatized her and made her feel inferior. Younger Jayd was the unbelonging– that is, that she didn't fit into the puzzle that was life. She was the one bruised apple in a pile of perfect ones, she was the pencil that was turned upside down when the rest of the stack were upright, and she was the one bent over flower in a bunch as they all stood up proudly in vase.

Younger Jayd just didn't *fit*. And her imaging made it worse, because it created and encased her into a world where she communicated with no one, but had sketched out their lives. This lack of connection and extreme observation made her uncomfortable and distrustful of everyone. And most of all, younger Jayd often wished she were dead.

Molly was behind Paul. She had slid into view and was making ugly faces behind him and mocking him as he spoke. I turned my attention back to him.

"We were engaged for about a year and was set to get married this September."

I looked up from his lips and into his eyes. He stared off into the distance and all I could see was a sea of honey in a dream like trance.

Then he suddenly snapped out of his thoughts.

"But, enough about me, Ashley. I'm being so rude. What about you? What is your family like? You look pretty young, but are married?"

Paul took a sip of his coffee and sat it back down on the dish. This cafe was a little gem. My latte was delicious, the best I've ever had. And the scenery inside the cafe was adorable; the interior resembled a cottage.

"No…I'm nineteen" I stuttered, not really knowing why I was doing so.

Paul looked surprised.

"Wow! You are young!" he exclaimed. "Nineteen. What an age. Prime of your life! What was I doing at nineteen? Hmmm…I believe I had started my business school program, already joined my fraternity and had met Melanie by then."
He went on about his time at business school and all the networking and connections he made. I thought back to when I first spotted Paul at the hospital. He was dressed in a tailored suit and had a large expensive looking watch on. He looked so professional and elite. He walked with

confidence and ambition in every step.

But I knew better.

"So, what did *you* want to be?" I asked him, gently interrupting him.

His eyes slowly widened as a hint of shock and confusion washed over his face. The question clearly caught him off guard, but he understood, as after a few moments, his face gradually softened and he gave that small sad smile of his. He took a few more moments to answer, as if deciding how best to explain.

"I honestly...could never pin it down to one thing, Ashley." he said. He took another sip of coffee before he continued.

"First there was this odd interest in geology that I had when I was a kid. I swore that I would grow up to be a geologist. Then I wanted to be a firefighter around the time I entered middle school, but mom thought that I could do better than a blue color job and pushed me towards finance and accounting. My dad wasn't really around, but he had been a firefighter. I think she just didn't want me to resemble him in any way. By high school I played around with possibly getting into biology and then law. Finally, I settled on business."

"But..." he quipped. "My true passion and hobby...will always be rocks. Thanks for asking."

I paused for a moment and then grinned. Our eyes met and we held each other's gaze. I quickly looked away. An unrecognizable feeling was stirring in me and I didn't like the way it made me feel. It made me feel seen…and vulnerable. I looked down at my empty cup, having finished my latte. I don't know how I would gather the strength and bravery to tell Paul the truth.

At that moment, my phone buzzed inside my jean pocket. I reached down and glanced at it. It was Mama. Unlocking it immediately I put the phone to my ear and got up from the table. I motioned to Paul that I had to take a call and he nodded.

"Mama…?" I said quietly, walking away from my seat to a corner in the cafe. "What's wrong?"

"Jayd!" Mama exclaimed in both disbelief and excitement. "You won't believe this!"

"What?" I asked her, worryingly. "What happened?"

"Oh baby! I can't believe it! Someone paid for your medical bills. I just got a call from the hospital. All of your bills have been paid off! Someone came by and paid for it in full!"

As Mama spoke her words sounded foreign to my ears. I glanced back at the table where Paul sat. He was looking down at his cup, back in his dream like trance. Molly stood behind him with her arms crossed. She looked pissed. Very pissed.

Chapter 24

"Gemini? no! Maybe an Aries?" I pondered out loud.

"Nope!" Paul smirked. "Try again!"

"Ugh…I don't know!" I said in annoyance, giving up at this game. Paul laughed out loud and I playfully groaned. Our eyes met and I peered deeply into his. It was silent before I spoke again, but I knew the right answer.

"Leo!" I told him. "You're a Leo!"

"There you go!" he laughed. "You got it! Finally"

We were back in Central Park, sitting at the very same bench we met days ago. I told Mama I was headed out to meet with Janelle and then go to work. I did both of those things, but as usual lately, Paul showed up at my job and asked if we could hang out. I said yes, this time. Not just because Sylvia once again pushed me out the door with Paul, but because I generally found Paul to be a chill guy.

"Ok!" I teased. "What's mine? Since you know so much about astrology!"

He looked directly into my eyes. If his eyes could swallow my own, they would have done so. Watery honey eyes peered into mine

"Pisces" he finally said, after some time. "You're a Pisces, Jayd."

I sat motionless and silent, puzzled at how he instantly knew. I looked down at the table, then quickly back up at him again. I gave him a smile.

"Yeah," I said. "Wow, you are good. How did you know?"

"Lucky guess?" he smirked. Silence hovered between us again.

Rays of sunlight spilled through the trees. A few red, yellow, and orange leaves blew through the streets as they fell from the trees. Birds perched on the park gates and on top of building ledges. A black and white stray cat walked on the sidewalk. I watched it run and hide under a parked car as approaching people walked nearby. The air was cool and the streets were emptier than the weeks before as Fall was finally here. Taking in the scene and the people, I dug my hands into the earth behind me and threw my head back, taking in deep breaths.

A few moments passed before I felt the skin of his hand under mine and realized I had put my own on top of his. My head snapped in his direction and I looked at him, expecting him to be just as horrified.

Instead, Paul looked straight ahead at the passing scene below, a small smile on his lips. It was like he didn't even notice. Shockingly, it dawned on me that I hadn't removed my hand off of his. Was I still in disbelief? Maybe I knew if I did remove my hand, he would look over and it would draw attention to what was happening.

So, I looked back at the street and tried to take my mind off of the situation. The silence was daunting and ever present now.

Molly appeared near the park's gate far off in front of us. She was doing cartwheels and trying to scare away the birds. But they didn't see her, so she gave up. Her eyes shifted towards me and she smiled. She began waving frantically and then stopped suddenly. With a quick motion of her hand, she clasped her neck in one hand and grasped at the air with the other. Gurgling and gasping sounds spewed from her throat as she struggled to breathe.

I looked at her in complete confusion, until I saw that sinister glimmer in her eyes. She was mocking me. She was pretending to drown. I looked away from Molly in disgust. Flitters of laughter rang in my ears.

Jayd, I heard her say. *How did it feel Jayd? You and Melanie? Did I get it right?*

My mind turned back towards the man I was sitting next to on the bench. He was peering over at me in concern.

"Are you okay, Ashley?" Paul asked.

"Yeah, I'm fine!" I quickly said. I looked down at the ground and the park walk path in front of us.

A boy on a skateboard rode by. Dogs being led on leashes and groups of people chatting walked in every direction. When he spoke, I had just been about to analyze the emotions of the entire scene.

Why couldn't life always be this simple as the surface level of it had us believe? Underneath the facade of a busy city lived a misery in each and every one of us. We were in constant competition to measure up and just to live our everyday lives. The woman walking her dog may very well have an abusive partner at home and she keeps that information from family and friends. Underneath her shades she may have a black eye. The little boy walking with his family and annoying his mother does so because he feels ignored and unloved by her. He desperately wants her attention but she takes his behavior as naughtiness. The teen girls walking and laughing together are actually laughing at one of their fellow classmates. They're cyber bullying her and mocking her photos. The couple grabbing a bite to eat at the food cart hate each other, but they stay together for appearances and family expectations.

There exists a darkness underneath the light, airiness of life. A silent, cruel darkness that played with humanity on puppet strings. Earth was the stage, and humanity the puppets. We played our parts while being controlled by the forces of society. I felt it in everyone I passed by. Anxiety and misery. Constantly running on a hamster wheel to get somewhere, and never reaching that place. And those who did reach it, realized in the end that the chase was never worth it. So, they withdraw and sulk until they crumble into dust.

It took me some time to come to this painful realization, but when I did accept it, it hurt less when I had to experience it. I think about all the ills of the world that occur, and how I'm powerless to stop them. I think about my insignificance in a vast, timeless space, and the impact I will leave on Earth. An Earth that will keep on spinning long after we are all gone. And there would be no one left to remember us.

And it will be as if our lives never existed. Why was the point? Does anyone look deeper than what they were being shown? Why does no one care?

Of course not Jayd, because people aren't weird losers who think about things like this.

Molly wasn't completely wrong as she whispered in my ear. Worst of all was that my mind was constantly preoccupied with thoughts of my existence and reality. Imaging came naturally to me like breathing and my attachment to feel everything never took a break. No…Molly wasn't completely wrong, and I hated that.

It was suffocating me.

And I found it unbelievably frustrating.

Why couldn't life be like a beautiful stock photo? To be observed and admired, and not questioned. It exists just because we need a subject that displays the type of life we desired, not what it actually was. But why couldn't it be like that? Is there a God, and what is he doing? Was this all for his amusement? Why was I still allowed to be here?

I bet Melanie didn't think of the things that I thought of. No, surely, she enjoyed life, just being happy that she was here at all. Melanie set off to and achieved at carving her mark into the world and leaving behind people who actually loved and missed her. At least she had that.

Meanwhile, what the hell was I doing?

I was aware that Paul was looking over at me. I felt his eyes on me. I wonder what he was thinking. Was he weirded out that I had been silent for so long? Was he thinking how plain I looked, how odd I acted, and how pathetic I was? Did he want to get up and leave? Maybe he was thinking of Melanie and comparing me to her. Of how chatty and lively she was compared to me and how much he missed her.

"You know, Ashley," he began, as I jumped in surprise at his voice. "I actually really enjoy this. My days lately have been so busy at the office and any time I can get away is a blessing. The world has a lot of beauty in it, and if we had the time to always sit back and take a look at it all, we'd really appreciate every day we have on Earth. Thank you for hanging out with me."

I didn't respond because I didn't have to. Paul moved his hand from under mine and then clasped my hand, squeezing it. I squeezed it back.

So, he *was* thinking about the beauty of the facade that was before us, after all.

Butterflies fluttered in my stomach when we left the park that day. Mol-ly was frowning as she walked behind us and I couldn't care less. I was living in this moment. Living in this facade.

Chapter 25

Jayd where are you going? What are you doing? Miss Myers asked me.

Hahahahaha! The other children laughed.

Quiet! Miss Myers shouted to the children. The children went quiet.

Miss Myers turned back to me.

I asked you a question, Jayd. Her tone was stern.

I didn't answer. Maybe because I didn't know what was wrong this time. Was it the methodical laughter from the other kids running around?

Was it the pissing in the corners and the stench of vomit that made my stomach turn?

Was it the crying from the kids that missed mommy and daddy and wanted to go home?

Or was it the crying from kids that were scared of mommy and daddy and had the bruises as evidence?

Was it the more extroverted kids who bullied the introverted ones?

Was it the sadness in the eyes of the kids that came to school hungry, dirty, and neglected?

Was it the spoiled kids who flaunted their new shoes or dresses in front of the less fortunate ones?

Or was it the teachers who complimented those kids and publicly favored them while scolding others?

Was it the pinching, pulling, or tagging when playing games?

Was it the wails and moans during nap time that reflected the kids' nightmares?

Was it all of these things and the fact that I felt it all so intensely?

Or was it simply me?

Little Jayd didn't. Little Jayd never knew.

Miss Myers couldn't see what I saw or feel what I felt.

Jayd, Miss Myers said coolly. Sit down now!

Hahahahahahaha!

Jayd! Miss Myers yelled again. I said sit down!

Hahahahahahaha!

But I didn't sit down. I stood up and walked briskly to the door.

Tears streamed down my cheeks!

I want my Mama! I cried as I ran out the door. I don't want to feel it anymore!

Jayd! Miss Myers shouted. Come back here!
Hahahahahahaha!

I said be quiet! Miss Myers shouted to the classroom.

Mama came later. She picked me up from under a table.

Wrapped in her arms, she cooed to me and swayed me back and forth.

I don't know what's wrong with your daughter, Ruby. Miss Myers shook her head.

Is it autism?

No! Mama said. Jayd's not autistic!

Are you sure? She has been acting up since she started the school year. Walking out of class, talking to herself, staring off into space, isolating herself from the other kids…

Is it ADHD? Miss Myers asked. I've known a few students who've been diagnosed with it.

No! Mama said. Jayd doesn't have ADHD! There's nothing wrong with her. She's just sensitive to her surroundings. You shouldn't shout at her.

Ruby, I have twenty other kids in this classroom. I can't be expected to look after Jayd all the time. You need to look into getting Jayd some help before she gets worse as she ages.

Mama glared at Miss Myers and stormed out of the room with me in her arms. That was my last day at that school before being homeschooled until the first grade.

"Hmm…" Janelle mused. She twirled her pen in her hand before scribbling down something on her clipboard.

The office seemed clearer today. All of the usual books and files that cluttered Janelle's desk were gone. There were more photos of artwork by her clients, however, that stood neatly in a square lining the edges of her desk.

"I think I can see a correlation from the time you were younger to what you display now in young adulthood."

Janelle crossed one leg over the other and laid her clipboard on her lap. She looked over at me, peering intently as she usually did.

"There's a repeated pattern of you being an outsider looking in. You feel victimized and confused by everything. Your mother was right, you are sensitive to your surroundings, Jayd. But the degree of your sensitivity goes beyond just feeling. There's a psychological connection with the way you perceive the world and the way it is. And then there is, of course, the way others perceive the world and in turn how they perceive and respond to you."

"You sometimes see it as a gift, but more than often, a curse. You may think that you're blessed in this day in age to be able to analyze people. Keeps you from potential danger and from getting yourself hurt." Janelle scribbled something down before she continued. "However, you wonder why it is that you have to be made aware of these things. Why do you, as fascinating as it can be, have to wonder about the meaning of life and everything in it. You wonder why you aren't allowed to just live. You wonder why you aren't allowed to feel your own feelings."

"You often get your feelings and the feelings of others mixed up. It's overwhelming for you and you wonder why you can't just live in the moment and feel only what you feel. This causes you anxiety and depression. It makes you an outcast and I believe has stunted your growth and ability to truly express yourself. So, you withdraw into a cocoon and miss out on the world as it passes you by."

"People tend to either aggressively zero in on you, or completely avoid you. Your rigidness and anxiety make them uncomfortable. Your ability to see through people, feel what they're feeling, and to a degree envision what and when something occurs makes you a mystery to others. They can't understand you."

"But you don't want to be a mystery. You don't want to observe and analyze all the time. You don't want to feel and empathize, do you Jayd? The very core of your being is being an empath, and this is what you believe causes all of your problems. Did I get that right, Jayd?"

I answered her with a nod, because if I spoke my voice would crack and Janelle would know that I was about to cry. It took great effort to force the tears back, because when everything was laid out in front of you and there was nowhere to hide, it was unbearable.

"Jayd…" Janelle continued, leaning forward, "you told me about your imaging and how you do it. You understand how, but what you're avoiding to address is why. Why do you image others, Jayd?"

Silence.

"It's ok to answer Jayd," Janelle said. "I just want to understand"

My hand was on my chin with my palm covering my mouth to hide that it was quivering. I took a deep breath and spoke quickly.

"I guess…I guess because it's a way I can put an identity to people I don't feel connected to.

"Yes!" Janelle exclaimed. "You feel disconnected to those around you! So, you create these back stories and scenarios to feel as if you are a part of their reality and to fill up a part of you that feels empty and alone inside. You're sick and tired of looking in from the outside, and imaging helps you, or rather makes you feel as if you have an understanding, or even some sort of control in the situation. And if you understand and are a part of reality, then you're not a freak, a loser, or whatever they call you."

They couldn't be contained now. Tears streamed down my cheeks and I didn't bother to wipe them away. Helping or not, I wanted to let Janelle see what she was doing to me.

She reached under her desk and pulled out a box of tissues. I took one and lazily wiped away the tears.

"I told you, Jayd, I'm not going to coddle you. What I want you to understand is that I can see where your depression stems from. You cannot run away from it."

Janelle continued to scribble on her clipboard. I peeked up and eyed her as she swiftly wrote something down. She spoke while writing.

"And what I also want you to understand is that You are not responsible for how other people perceive you. How they react and what they think and feel is not something that should upset you or even concern you at all. Let that be their burden to hold."

"Jayd, you possess the unique ability to do what many can't, and that isn't something to be ashamed or hide from. What you need to do is work with who you are, not resist it. Fighting against how you naturally perceive the world and everything in it does your mental health no favors. You need to be kinder and more patient with yourself. There is nothing wrong with you, Jayd."

I didn't know how I could accept that. There had to be something wrong with me. It couldn't just be explained away like that. It wasn't that easy. I wanted Janelle to give me the remedy. I wanted Janelle to give me the cure. The normally large and airy room suddenly felt small. Janelle's words had opened up a part of me that I preferred to keep closed. And hidden.

"I met up with Paul...again," I hesitantly began, not knowing exactly how I would explain to Janelle that I didn't do as she had suggested.

"We hung out a few times," I told her. "He's nice…"

Janelle furrowed her eyebrows and squinted her eyes at me. She wanted me to say more.

"We hung out at a cafe. Then a park. He's a very interesting guy. Successful, works in Manhattan, and he's very active.

Janelle's face didn't alter. She was waiting for me to reveal whether or not I told Paul who I was.

"He's very easy to talk to; a very friendly guy that just wants someone else to connect with."

Janelle continued to eye me intently.

"He invited me to go see a play with him. I told him I would think about it."

"Why, Jayd?" Janelle asked. Her tone indicated that she knew what I was dodging. "Why not go to the play with him?"

"I don't really like plays," I told her. "I'm more of a movie person."

"So, suggest a movie that the two of you could see," Janelle said.

"There's nothing out right now that interests me," I told her, quickly.

"Then suggest something else. Go hiking or boating. Go to a concert or an amusement park."

"I guess…" I began, "But I don't know if I really have the time and-"

"Jayd," came a stern voice. Janelle sounded so similar to Miss Myers. "We talked about this, Jayd. You cannot keep running from your problems. You and Paul, through unfortunate circumstances, have a connection whether you like it or not. Melanie was his fiancé and I'm sure he's suffering just as much as you are."

"I'm not asking you to take the responsibility for what happened to Melanie." Janelle said, leaning forward again. "Let me be clear, that was not your fault."

"But you must take responsibility for the fact that it did happen, and that you need to acknowledge it."

"Jayd, you tried to commit suicide. A woman died out in that water attempting to save you. A woman who had a life and loved ones. Don't you think Paul should at least know the girl who his late fiancé risked her life and died for? You really don't think you at least owe him that?"

Truthfully, I didn't think I owed anyone anything.

Except Melanie. I owed her my life.

Yet every time we came face to face, I was awash with guilt. Paul was so courteous and kind, and didn't even know I was his fiancé's killer. What would he think of me if he found out now? Would he think that I was twisted and sick for not revealing myself and then befriending him? Would he sympathize with me or would he never want to see me again? Would he fly off in a fit of rage? He loved Melanie, and from the way his face lit up when he talked about her, Paul had truly lost his other half.

Who could I say I loved that much? Mama? I don't know what I would do if Mama was ever taken away from me. I couldn't think of what I'd do. It was unimaginable.

Was I really keeping Paul from getting closure? Was he out there wondering who I was and when I would be revealed?

"Someone paid for my medical bills, but we don't know who." I said to Janelle, desperately wanting to switch the subject to something else. "They paid off all of them completely. I wonder if it was him?"

Janelle had been watching me as I pondered my situation with Paul, but now her face lit up.

"Jayd, that's wonderful!" she exclaimed. "I know that was a huge burden for your family."

"And yes, it wouldn't surprise me if Paul was the one who did so…" she continued. "Like I said Jayd, Paul, just like you, needs closure."

We talked a bit more about my job and whether I was preparing to go to college in the fall before I left and headed over for my shift at Sylvia's Before leaving Janelle's office, Molly whispered in my ear that I should stop going to Janelle and that she only gave me false hope. I pushed past her in frustration, cursing the day she ever appeared in my life.

I couldn't fix what I did. I couldn't go back in time and change things no matter how much I wanted to. And that was the bitter pill I forced myself to gulp down.

Chapter 26

Passion and pain emanated from her very soul. Her movements were graceful and sharp. They were clumsy and erratic. They were powerful and muted. Her voice was scratchy in the beginning as she belted out her monologue, but now she liberated, she sang with a voice so ethereal and angelic. Her voice echoed across the room and bounced off the walls until it graced our ears. She twirled around the stage, dodging the props until she came to a sudden halt. The entire room had gone silent.

Her lover had now come up behind her and gripped her hands. He began to twirl and sing to her. They danced in perfect unison and harmony. He rocked back and forth and stomped and shouted and she did the same. She spun and yelled out to the crowd and he did the same. The background daytime sky had now changed to night and the couple's voices had begun too lower. The stage emptied of the many props until it was only the lovers left. They stood in the middle of the stage and quietly sung to each other until their voices had quieted to a whisper. The crowd all seemed to lean forward as they gazed upon the two. This was it. This was their final moments together before their tragic end. With dreaded anticipation, we all listened for the sound of the soldiers coming. And when their stomping could finally be heard, the couple whose voices could barely be heard now, had stopped singing and looked toward their left. The stomping continued and loud angry voices could be heard. Moments later, a loud bang rang out and echoed off of the walls. The couple turned to each other, gripping each other tightly and looked into each other's eyes one last time. Tears streamed down their faces, but their expressions were happy. They were glad that they would at least be able to die together. With one final gaze into each other's eyes, their lips locked as the soldiers shouted at them and closed in for the kill.

And then the curtains rapidly closed.

There was silence in the room at first, and then only moments later, it erupted in applause. People from the balconies and way up in front stood up and slapped their hands together. Shouting and cheers roared throughout the room. The noise in this theater was louder than any music I blasted through my headphones. I could feel the admiration, shock, and enjoyment by everyone here. And as usual, it was overwhelming.

Paul and I stood up as well and clapped our hands. We were both impressed and we didn't even need to tell each other that. I could feel his energy so strongly. He wore his usual dress suits when we went on our fancier outings and I wore my usual shirt, sneakers, and jeans. Paul never seemed to mind. Later the cast came back for a final applause and bow, and not more than five minutes after, Paul and I were outside on the sidewalk, walking and talking about the show.

"So, what did you think?" Paul asked.

He had asked me the same thing after each show we saw and I always gave him the same answer.

"I thought it was great!" I told him, really meaning it. "Although they were only acting, you could feel their emotion strongly. They did a really good job!"

We walked on and continued to talk as Paul led the way. We were going to a restaurant now, just like we did after every show. My stomach growled as I thought about sitting down and enjoying a delicious meal. I made sure to skip lunch earlier and Paul always treated me to the best restaurants. We walked down the block, side by side with Paul ahead. He had one arm in his pocket and another arm looped into my arm. It had taken me some time to get used to that level of touch, but after a few times I had concluded that it wasn't a romantic gesture, but a friendly platonic one.

It was beautiful out tonight. The wind was still and not a single leaf ruffled or blew. Stars shone brightly above- a rarity for New York City. Bright lights from buildings and loud chatter from crowds of people surrounded us as we walked on. It was still smelly and cluttered, as it typically was. But the ambiance and energy were so lively and positive that I could overlook it.

There were so many people out tonight and Paul and I had to dodge and weave in and out of so many crowds. We were now blocks away from the theater and into the heart of the city.

"I'll hail us a cab!" Paul said. "The place is a bit aways from here. It's a really good place. You'll love it. I've been here many times before."

Paul walked to the edge of the sidewalk and into the street and began waving his arms. It only took a few moments before we were noticed and a taxi leaped from the traffic and honked at us. Cabs usually never stopped when I tried to hail them. I guess they thought I looked too shabby and miserable to pick up. We hurried over to the cab and got inside. Paul directed the driver on where to go and off we went.

"Y 'know Ashley, I have a love-hate relationship with New York." he said, turning to me. "New Yorkers can be rude and uppity, but there is a silent unity here. And there's so much to do and see. I'll never get tired of it!" I nodded in agreement with him. New York was the only place I knew to call home.

"So, when are you going to start going back to the group sessions?" Paul suddenly asked me.

The question caught me off guard as I gazed out the window at all the traffic and lights. I slowly turned to him in confusion before I understood what he meant. He smiled softly at me as he waited for my answer. When I didn't respond, he continued to talk.

"It has really ramped up since you stopped going, Ashley. The group has really gotten to know each other better. The support we all give to each other and receive is amazing. I believe so much healing is happening. People are opening old childhood wounds, things they experience daily, and their inner thoughts and trauma that they would have previously never told a soul."

I was now looking over at him as he spoke. "We all have been through so much and it's great that we can all come together and get the support that we need. It's opened my eyes to the fact that while many of us don't seem to be going through something on the outside, we often harbor so much pain inside. It was great to just be there and listen to everyone. That's really all many of the people there needed. Someone to listen to them and offer support."

I watched him as he talked about the group that I had long abandoned and had no intentions of returning to. I slowly turned away and looked back outside the window.

"I don't think I'm interested in any more group sessions Paul," I told him. "I'm sorry"

Silence drifted between us and I could tell the driver was now peeking into our conversation.
I didn't care, as I had nothing but the truth to tell Paul. And right now, that truth had been burning in the back of my head since I first laid eyes on him.

"They don't ever seem to solve my issues," I told him, wanting to fill in the awkward silence that fell between us. I felt Paul wanting me to go on and explain, so I would. It was the least I could do for killing his fiancé.

"I've been to therapists and group sessions before in the past. They never seemed to help much. My problems stem more from uncontrolled and suffocating emotions that I cannot avoid. Whereas others are diagnosed with autism or ADHD, I've been told my issue is being a severe empath. Feeling everything and everyone all at once until I can no longer connect with reality. Where I can no longer sit and function like a normal person. To where I'm overcome with emotion so much that I can't tell which is mine and which isn't."

"I've been like this since I was little Paul," I told him. "And it hasn't gotten any better. Only worse. I have a good therapist now. She tells me that I need to work with my uniqueness, instead of fighting it. I don't see that working at all, but I guess..."

Tears had begun to stream down my face, but I didn't feel any sadness. They slowly dripped along my cheek and off my chin. I felt nothing inside. Paul squeezed my hand for comfort, but I knew nothing could comfort me. Not even Mama right now. It was a nice gesture on his part though.

I don't really know why I was being so open with Paul right now. Did I trust him? Did I feel guilty about Melanie and wanted him to at least know something that was the truth about myself? Or was it because I simply no longer cared to keep it to myself anymore? We rode on in silence and about thirty minutes later, we stopped outside one of the most upscale looking restaurants I had ever seen. It was a white and blue Grecian style building with gold vases lining each column. All around the front of the building were stunning flowers planted.

Paul and I got out of the cab, Paul paid the driver, and we headed towards the restaurant entrance. Neither of us spoke as we made our way inside. Once in, I gazed around. I was just as stunned by the beauty of the outside of the building as I was by the inside. Gold drapes lined the outer pillars and columns, and every window had silky blue curtains. Each table in the restaurant had a bouquet of flowers in the middle. There was a second floor of tables and there was a massive chandelier hanging down from the ceiling in the center of the room.

Paul informed the pretty, brunette hostess that we had a reservation and she quickly took out menus and ushered us to the second floor and to a private seating area.

As we sat down, a waiter promptly came over and brought a bread basket and pitcher of water. He was a tall and handsome Mediterranean man and his name was Jacob. He took our orders for drinks and I asked for an ice tea, knowing that I really wanted a glass of wine but that I was underage and they would ask for my ID.

Paul ordered a bourbon. The waiter left to fulfill our order and Paul turned to me. He rested his hands on the tables and looked me straight in the eyes.

"Ashley," he began, in a quiet tone. "I didn't mean to pry or push you into going to the group sessions. I just thought they would help since they're helping so many people. They are...helping me..."

My response to him was silence as he trailed off. Not because I was upset, but because I truly had nothing to say. I had told him the truth and inner turmoil that had been plaguing me all my life. And I felt completely trapped by it all. I hated the notion of spoiling this wonderful evening for Paul and I, so I tried to change the subject.

"I might be going to school later this fall.," I told him. "I'm not sure what I'll be majoring in as I haven't picked out any programs or classes yet. But with my job and a little extra money coming in, my parents thought I should start..." It was not entirely true. I still didn't want to go, and Mama was the only parent I had. But with my hospital bills miraculously being paid off, there was now more extra money coming from my job and Mama was pushing me to apply.

Paul didn't respond, though. He was looking down at the napkin that sat beside his plate. His honey-colored eyes were hazy, as if he were falling back into that dreamlike state of his. His expression was without any ounce of emotion, just thought. Deep into hidden thoughts. The sudden change startled me.

"I'm getting promoted at my job," I told him, seeing if he would come back. Promotion was a bit of a stretch. Sylvia just wanted me to organize some shipments that she would now be receiving and had finally given me access to the back storage. I was still being paid the same.

Paul still didn't respond to me. He continued to look down at his napkin. I wonder what he was thinking. His expression was like he was in a trance, but just bursting to say something. To yell out something that was deep inside and troubling him.

"Early fall is coming up soon!" I said in a desperate attempt to snap him out of his trance. "I love the fall season! What about you?"

Still nothing. He looked completely gone now. Stuck in his mind thinking about something. He was probably thinking about Melanie. I bet they used to go out to upscale restaurants like this and sit and chat in private seating. It was all coming back to him now. How much he missed her and how much he'd rather be here with her than some strange, miserly, average looking girl. It was stupid of me to agree to do this. Why couldn't I for once in my life *think* instead of *feel*? Poor Paul. I should have made an excuse to leave right when we pulled up.

Because, as much as I wished I didn't, I recognized this restaurant in one of Melanie's old photos online of her and Paul. The interior was identical. This was a huge mistake.

But how could I have known he would choose this place?

You knew Jayd. You just didn't care. You're sick.

Molly stood off to the far left of us, sitting on top of one of the balcony rails. She wore her usual baby doll dresses with matching ribbons in her hair. Dark circles and rough lines lined her youthful face. She looked so old and haggard. As much as I hated her, I couldn't bring myself not to at least wonder or care even a little about what was wrong with her. It was like she was morphing into something broken and decrepit.

Something that was rapidly crumbling before my eyes. But I couldn't worry about that right now. I turned away and tried to ignore her and reluctantly looked back at Paul. Lightheadedness began to creep up on me and I felt my eyes fill up with water although no tears fell this time.

I was seconds away from shouting at him to just pour out what was on his mind when he finally spoke up.

"We were arguing the day she...died." I froze and looked at him through watery eyes, listening.

"In the car that day she saw that girl on the bridge," he said sullenly. "We had been arguing all morning."

"I had decided to call off the wedding that day, and we were driving to tell her parents the news." We got into an argument and as we were stuck in that traffic on the bridge, she got out and yelled that she'd rather walk the rest of the way. She slammed the door shut and was headed straight forward before we heard that there was loud commotion going on to our right. At the right edge of the bridge, a crowd was gathering. It was stormy that day, and hard to tell what people were shouting. Many people were yelling and screaming out the side of their windows. I thought I heard someone say to call the police, someone else scream to stop her, and another person yell that it was too late. Melanie stood still, looking at the crowd. I was looking over there as well. I remember wanting to tell her to get back into the car, a storm was approaching."

But, when we both got a clear look at what the crowd were all yelling about, I could see that there was a girl on the side of the bridge all the way to our right, leaning over, arms outstretched, and preparing to jump."

I sat listening to him, keeping my face neutral. I'm not sure if it was for me or for him, but I wasn't feeling anything at the moment. I was just taking each and every word in, letting it simmer in my brain before moving on to the next. Numbness had washed over me as he reiterated that horrible day.

"Melanie saw the girl, and immediately jumped into action, dodging and weaving in and around cars. I couldn't catch up to her, nor would she listen to my shouts, telling her to stop. To wait. To hold on."

"She was headstrong and brave, Ashley. She was selfless and generous. She was a wonderful human being. But in the end, it wasn't enough for fate to be kind to her. As the girl jumped, she grabbed onto her and they both went under. When I got to the edge, I saw neither emerge. It was so chaotic. I jumped up on the edge, ready to go in after them, but someone held me back. Several people were shouting at me as they held my arms and dragged me away. Screaming and crying all around. It was like a nightmare flashing before my eyes. I heard sirens in the distance and I was just begging for Melanie and the girl to be alive. For them to have made it. Melanie was an excellent swimmer. She had taken numerous safety classes. She would make it, I told myself. She would make it and save the girl."

Tears spilled down my cheeks as my watery eyes began to overflow. My body felt hot and a ringing in my ears grew. I knew the story well. I was one of the main characters and as Paul sat here and recalled everything, I couldn't help but to wonder if I was having a nightmare myself. Was I actually sitting here and hearing all of this?

My nostrils and throat seemed to close and fill up with water while a burning sensation erupted in my head. My chest pounded as my lungs filled up with water and my body sunk as I thrashed about wildly. I was choking and drowning again. All over again. Paul went on and it took so much in me to continue to sit and listen.

"But she didn't, Ashley. She didn't. She didn't make it. And I could only tell myself that it was my fault that day. Because if I had never called off the wedding, we would never have been there on that bridge. If I hadn't called off the wedding, Melanie would have never been upset and stormed out of the car."

"We were going to Switzerland. I was going to take her there as an engagement present before I decided that it was best if we parted ways. Switzerland. Melanie always wanted to go to Switzerland. But I couldn't keep up the lies and the charades anymore because the truth was that I didn't love her. I loved the idea of her when we first got together and I loved her like a family member, but I wasn't in love with her. I'm not sure if I ever did. I'm not sure if it was that I liked the idea of Melanie and the idea of us together, but I had just one day come to the conclusion that I wasn't in love with her. Maybe it was mine and everyone's expectation that the successful young college sweethearts get married. I don't know anymore. I didn't realize this until after we were engaged, and I knew that I had fucked up proposing to her. That I would break her heart. I have no one to blame but myself. I loved her. She was my best friend. And I killed her, Ashley. I killed her."

Paul was choking my tears and his voice was quivering.

Why was he doing this to himself? I thought. I suppose he needed to get it all out, but he was torturing himself just as much as he was torturing me. Poor Melanie. To find out that the love of her life never loved her, but only as a friend.

"Melanie and I were alike in many ways, but we were so different. And we wanted different things out of life. I just wish I could have saved her that day. She deserved to live her life and accomplish her dreams. But I got in the way of that. I killed her, Ashley. I killed her and her dreams."

No, you didn't. I did.

Paul and I sat there for what seemed like eternity. Neither of us spoke as I guess neither of us had more to say. Jacob came back to take our orders and Paul quietly ordered for the both of us. When Jacob left, Paul stood up from the table. I glanced up at him, thinking he had to excuse himself to go to the restroom, but instead he reached into his coat pocket and pulled out a small, silky red gift box. My heart stopped when I saw it and I quickly looked up at Paul in shock and confusion.

What was he doing?

"Ashley, I brought you something," Paul said as he sat back down and slid the box over to me. "A little gift I picked up this afternoon. It reminded me of you. It's a little thanks for being a great friend to me. For being someone that is nice enough to just sit and listen. I haven't met very many people like that. So, thank you."

He looked me in the eyes and we held each other's gaze for a moment. I didn't get a feeling of romantic interest from Paul, but there was something hidden in his eyes instead. Looking down at the beautiful little box, I put one hand forward and gently touched it. It was so soft that I was completely sure it was wrapped in real silk. I untied the bow around the box and opened it.

And that was it. At that very second, I had had enough, and knew that he knew. It was a joke. A cruel, cruel, joke. A well-played joke. A joke that I suppose I deserved as I floated throughout the days trying to absolve myself of the guilt that I felt. Of the pain that wouldn't leave me. I was a clown at a circus, and Paul was one of the many in the audience. All this time he knew, and it was the most heartbreaking thing of it all.

Sitting inside of the box on a miniature, silk cushion was a small, neatly cut, jade gemstone.

In a flurry I was on my feet and out of the restaurant door. I didn't bother looking back at Paul. I was sure he was still sitting there. Still thinking about Melanie and how I ruined it all and how he got caught up in it. Paul may have called off the wedding, but it was me who was present on that bridge that day.

I ran down the steps and down the street, not knowing where I was going, but knowing I had to get out of there.

"Jayd! Wait!" came a voice far behind me now. But I didn't stop. I couldn't stop. My legs had a mind of their own and my head was spinning with a million thoughts. I could feel Molly trailing me. I'm so sorry Paul. I'm so sorry Melanie. I shouldn't be here. It's really all my fault.

Yes, Jayd. Now you see. Now you finally see it…

Chapter 27

A ball of fluff and fur sat beside me and laid on my stomach. I stroked its head and cheeks while humming a long forgotten tune.

My room was a complete mess. Clothes lay on the floor and dressers and drawers were wide open. My bag and some furniture were tucked in the corner. The lights were off and the window was shut tightly. Above me I tried to listen in on the loud shouting of a couple that I called The Divided. I called them this because as long as I could remember, everyone who moved above my room was always arguing and yelling at each other. Sometimes they were physical fights and the police had to be called.

The Divided were from all walks of life. A childless couple, a married couple, siblings and roommates. Most recently, a young childless couple had moved in and had been arguing ever since. I really didn't need to do imaging with them to know about their lives– they shouted out their business for the entire building to hear. However, I did try to fill in the blanks.

He was always out late and possibly cheating, she thought. She was overbearing and clingy. He didn't help with housework but wanted to continue being 50-50 with finances and she didn't think this was fair. He wanted her to be a working housewife and she told him there was no such thing. She wanted to go back to school and he wanted children. They had already broken up over and over again and yet they always came back together.

I figured deep down inside they both simply lusted after each other and jumped into a relationship too quickly. He was immature and not ready for a serious relationship like her. She expected too much from him and knew that he wasn't the one for her from the beginning. She didn't think she had any other options while he thought he had all the options in the world. He wanted to tie her down and run the streets and she wanted a picture perfect family life. They were obviously not compatible. Yet they stayed together making each other miserable.

I didn't feel sorry for either of them and on this particular day, I really wished they both would shut the fuck up and be quiet for once.
Music drifted in from the way down below outside of my window. I felt tired, beaten, and depressed. I have no idea how I made my way back home, but I was still wearing my clothes from the day before and I was in my room somehow. I must have burst through my door and knocked things around before jumping into bed.

When I woke up this morning, I could hear Mama in the kitchen. I decided to stay home and skip work. My session with Janelle could wait as well. I needed time to process what was happening in my life right now.

Why are we created the way we are? Is it karma? Some kind of cruel joke? Or does everything happen by chance?

I've wondered this since I was a child, and no matter what adults would tell me, I still had my doubts about it all. *You're just unique Jayd, don't beat yourself up about it.* They would say. *You're special. You're different. It's a gift.* They would say. *There are kids out there that go through worse than you, Jayd. Stop complaining* They would say.

Why did it seem like bad things happened to good people? Or at least decent people? The world didn't seem to care at all. It just kept spinning. The seasons came and went. Life bloomed and then fizzled and died. The weak were conquered and the strong prevailed. Hope and dreams died, while a lucky few survived. And then the process would repeat itself.

You had one life to get it all right because there were no second chances. It didn't matter if you didn't ask to be born, you were here now and you had to play the game. Suck it up, buttercup.

What was the point of it all? What was the meaning of it all?

I shifted to my side and hugged Norman into my chest. Burying my face into his fur I let the tears fall as I quietly cried.

Why did she have to do it? Why did she have to try and save me? Why?

The world needed her more than it needed me!

Melanie was actually going places in life. She was actually helping people and accomplishing things I could never do. The tears seeped into Norman's fur and I listened to the methodical sound of his breathing.

My mind shifted to days long passed. Memories of when I was a lonely child. Curled up in a ball and breathing deeply no matter where I was. Teachers hated me and kids mocked me. My response to it all was silence.

I felt her before she even spoke. A deep aggravation in me rose. Go away, Molly. Go away forever.

It was all your fault Jayd. Everyone tried to help you but you simply couldn't be helped. Your Mama tried to help you but eventually she gave up because you're hopeless. You tried to block out everyone all the time. Block out the world. But it doesn't work that way.

I continued breathing in and out into Norman's fur. My breathing picked up and so did my tears.

Don't try to ignore me, Jayd. You know you can't. Hehehehehehe h!

Breathe in and out. In and out.

Paul knew all along. He knew it was you. He knew it was you and the whole truth exploded in your face! You thought you were keeping the truth from him but he played you like a fiddle! Hahaha! Tell me Jayd, how does that feel? You thought all along that the two of you were becoming great friends and that you could get away with not telling the truth. You thought you could keep up your lie forever and continue to use Paul for your own sick closure. But it didn't work! He knew you were a fake. He knew you had no shame, sitting there with him as if you did nothing! As if you didn't kill his fiancé!

In and out. In and out. I squeezed Norman tighter, digging my hands into his fur as Molly continued to lash out.
He hates you. They all do. And you deserve it. You embarrassed this family and ruined the lives of so many. I know you feel it, Jayd. I know you feel every bit of it. Aunt Opal was right about you and even your Mama knows she's right! She'll just never admit it!

My head slowly lifted out of the poor animal I was suffocating in my grip. I turned to Molly who was sitting down on the edge of my bed facing me with that large, disgusting grin on her face.
"I never told her to save me, Molly. I didn't tell her to jump in after me. She did that herself. I wanted to die that day. Now leave me alone!"

Well, someone had to save your pathetic ass, Jayd. Melanie was kind and heroic.

More than you could ever be. Someone had to be the brave one. It was unfortunate that it was such a great person that decided to waste their life on you."

Molly cupped her head in both of her hands and smiled at me.

I'm sure if Melanie knew what a loser you were, she wouldn't have jumped in after you. That crowd should have been cheering when you went over. One less loser in the world.

"Just shut up!" I yelled at her. "Shut the fuck up you demon!"

Hahahahaha!

"Jayd?!" I could hear Mama yell from in the kitchen. "Are you okay? What's going on?" I ignored Mama and continued yelling at Molly.

"Go away, Molly! I don't know where you came from but it's time for you to go away!"

Hahahaha!

I swung at her, and of course my hand went right through her. Molly wasn't real.

Hahahahahaha! Nice try, Jayd! Don't get mad at me for telling the truth! You're useless and you don't deserve to be here! You should have never been born! You're a waste of life and a waste of space! Everyone knows it! Even if you know it!

"I said shut up you evil fucking bitch!" I lunged at her repeatedly knowing I couldn't hurt her. Mama was now banging on my door and shouting but I couldn't make out what she was saying. I was enraged and thrashing and cursing and shouting. Molly laughed the entire time, rippling in and out of reality as my hands passed right through her. Mama kept on yelling and banging on the door.

It was like that until I was exhausted and finally passed out.

Chapter 28

Her arms were menacingly outstretched as she lifted her head and our eyes met. Her black hair was floating all around her face, concealing its lower half. She wasn't swimming, but rather seamlessly moving through the water. I couldn't tell if she was scowling or grinning, but either way, I knew she wanted to kill me.

It was dark and freezing under the water and I had no idea where I was. Cold water was filling my lungs and my eyes stung. My vision was becoming more unclear by the second, but I needed to keep my eyes on her as she crept closer to me. I flapped my arms and kicked my feet wildly, trying to reach the surface, but it was of no use. It was as if I was being held in place by an invisible force.

Hehehehehe! came a cruel voice in my head. Molly was somewhere nearby but I couldn't see her. A sudden force pulled me further down and a vicious scream erupted in the water. The menacing woman was getting closer. Two hands gripped my ankles and pulled me downwards as I tried fruitlessly to kick them off.

Hehehehehehe!

It was Molly. She was the one pulling me down and holding me into place.

Die, Jayd. Die!

Let me go! I shouted at her in my head, not daring to open my mouth and drown myself even further. My lungs felt as if they were ready to burst and the stinging pain in my head was unbearable. My body was numb and I couldn't feel my limbs anymore.

So, this was it, huh? So, this was how it would all end? I guess I shouldn't be surprised. I guess this is what was bound to happen. It was what I probably deserved. To die with no one but a monster and Molly to witness my last breath. To have never gotten closure or live my life for Melanie. To never see Mama again. Or drink at Pat's or work at Sylvia's. Or visit Janelle's office. They would mourn me after I was gone, but they would eventually move on and I would have been forgotten. A dead soul under the cold dark water. Alone and pitiful. It was what I deserved. And I accept my fate.

And what about Paul? Would he be happy to see me dead? Or would he care at all? Would he be satisfied that I suffered the same fate that I inflicted upon his fiancé?

The thrashing stopped as my limbs went still. My entire insides were now submerged in water. Consciousness was quickly fading and I welcomed death. I was tired and just wanted it all to end. I was sick of having to relive that day and sick of having to live each day afterwards. I welcome the stillness and darkness. The eternal loneliness. It wasn't like life was much different and I was used to it by now. And at least I wouldn't have to see or hear Molly anymore.

With the little sight I had left, I watched as the monster crept forward and then paused only a few feet away. Our eyes met once again and hatred and anger emanated from her. The hate and anger seemed to shroud her as it vibrated off of her body. Her aura was dark. Her energy was evil.

And then she lunged forward, right at me.

As her thin, wrinkled fingers wrapped around my neck, I weakly lashed out at her and managed to scrape back the hair from her face. It was then that I could see the monster's face. It was Melanie.

YOU KILLED ME! She screamed at me. YOU RUINED MY LIFE. YOU RUINED HIS LIFE!

No! I'm sorry! I wanted to yell, but I was far too weak to muster up a sound. My lashing out had ended as soon as it started. Melanie gripped me and pulled me downward as she continued to shout. We sunk further and further into the darkness.

YOU'RE A MURDERER! YOU TOOK MY LIFE! YOU DON'T DESERVE TO LIVE!

What a fitting end. To be drowned by the drowned.

And then like at every climax of a dream, I woke up from my nightmare in a pool of sweat and sat face up.

Norman had jumped up and flew off the bed in fright. I watched as he scurried underneath the bed and made sleepy, sad meows.

Heaving in and out I breathed heavily and listened. Nothing. The house was silent. I was in bed, alive, and safe. It was all a horrible, yet so realistic nightmare.

Streams of light shone through my bedroom window and I inhaled deeply. From one corner to the other, I looked around my room. Nothing.

And then there was a sound behind me. Dreading to look behind, I continued to face forward.

Swisshhh, the sound was louder this time. Immense fear washed over me and I went completely still.

C'mon now Jayd. You're hearing things.

It took a few moments to gather enough courage to turn around, and when I did it was exactly as I expected. Nothing. There was nothing behind me, or my bed, or on the wall.

I turned back around in both relief and frustration. I was just about to quickly lie back down before I saw her. Standing in the left corner of my room near the window was a large, dark figure hunched over and peering at me.

I choked on a scream as I realized what the figure was. Before I could react, the figure shifted into another person. This time it was Molly. A maniacal grin crossed her lips. And then Molly shifted back to the dark figure, who I recognized as the monstrous Melanie from my nightmare.

The dark figure made some kind of screech before she leered forward as if she was about to pounce. Then it switched back to Molly with that same awful smile on her face. Molly was moving erratically, as if she was being pulled in and out of reality. She began yelling, then laughing, then crying. And then it switched back to Melanie. Then Molly. Then Melanie. And again and again and again in rapid succession.

Die Jayd! The Melanie-Molly creature hissed. *You thought trying to live for me would fix what you did!? How pathetic! You could never live up to me! Even in death! I hate you! It's your fault I'm dead! I will avenge my death! And the only way to right this wrong is for you to die as well!*

I hurled myself off of my bed and scrambled to the door, knocking clothes and other items down. Norman flew out from under my bed and ran out of my room when I got the door open.

"Jayd?" I could hear Mama call out. "What's that noise?"

Mama, help! I wanted to shout, but the rapid switching and sounds of the creatures behind me seemed to drown out my voice.

In the very distant background from all the noise, I could hear knocking. Someone was at the door.

Run away! There are monsters here! I wanted to yell out but again my voice was muted by the noise.

Kill yourself, Jayd! Die! came a terrifying demonic voice from behind. I bolted out of my room and down the hall into the living room towards the front door.

"Jayd?" Mama said from the living room. "What's wrong? Where are you going?"

"I'm sorry, Mama!" The tears came down like heavy waterfalls as I spoke to my beautiful mother. "I can't do this anymore! I love you and I want you to always know that! It's not your fault! Goodbye Mama!

"What are you talking about, Jayd?!" Mama said, confused, worried, and alarmed all in one. She moved towards me, but I stepped back.

"I'm sorry for all the pain and frustration I've caused you! I'm sorry for even being born!" The words spilled out of me and I tried not to feel each one or linger on what I was conveying to her. I needed to make sure Mama heard me one last time.

"I've had enough. I'm not strong enough, Mama. I know what I have to do. I killed Melanie and even though she's gone, she's found a way to make sure she kills me back. I'm leaving you now, and I have to make sure I get it right this time. Goodbye, Mama."

"Jayd, baby, what are you saying?" Mama shrieked. "You're scaring me!?"

I grabbed open the front door and ran out, passing Paul who glanced at me with surprise and concern as I rushed past him. For a split second I wondered why he was at my door, so I quickly decided that it didn't even matter. Nothing mattered anymore.

"Jayd!!" Mama screamed. "Come back! Someone help! Please, oh God! Help!"

I tried to contain the overwhelming emotions that vibrated throughout my body. I felt angry, weak, and depressed. I felt brave, yet cowardly. I felt like nothing and everything. I felt liberated and relieved.

It was finally going to be over.

Chapter 29

I peddled through the wind like a bullet, dodging people who cried out in annoyance as I zoomed past them. Who cares if I upset them? I would never see them again and they would never know me. This was the end.

My legs felt like they were on fire as I continued to peddle non-stop. I was thinking and not thinking at the same time. I knew what I had to do and knew exactly where I was going. Traffic was particularly heavy and there was a bit of fog obstructing my view. The clouds were getting darker and the wind had picked up. The day was threatening to be rainy and dreary. It was as if fate knew and had aligned the perfect atmosphere for me. Again.

It was hard not to think about what I was going to leave behind. It pained me to leave Mama, Norman, and Pat. Janelle would be sad as she thought I was getting better and making progress. I hope she didn't blame herself. From the very beginning if she had known how hopeless it all was, she wouldn't have even bothered.

I don't know how long I had been peddling but I was nearing the bridge now. The bridge where it all happened. Manhattan was crowded and the bridge was full of honking, angry drivers. As I rode into Brooklyn, I sped past the drivers and to the spot. The spot that still had fake flowers and a now battered, weathered, teddy bear sat in remembrance. The spot where I went over the edge and another woman followed. The spot where a decision I made ruined the life of another. The spot where I came full circle back to. To finish what I started.

My bike came to a halt right at the spot. I tossed the bike to the side and scrambled over to the edge. Lifting one leg over the other, I moved my body over the upper rail and onto the edge of the bridge. I balanced my weight on the lower ledge and rested back against the giant metal structure. I could feel eyes looking out from cars on me. Never again would I have to feel their eyes and their auras. Never again would I have to feel anything.

Cars began honking their horns loudly, trying to get my attention or alert other cars. I had my back to everyone. The old world behind me full of despair and misery would be left behind. My new home was far below me, and it welcomed me with swishing waves.

I'm not sure what made me look up and back towards the way I came, but when I did, off in the distance, I could see the faint outline of a familiar man biking rapidly my way.

Of course, he made it here quickly.

In the midst of the chaos, I should've known he would come after me. Was it to push me over or try to stop me? Or did he just want to sit and watch? He didn't love Melanie, but maybe my death would give him closure. Or perhaps Paul wanted to join me in death, as his guilt about Melanie's death seemed to match mine. Whatever the reason was, I couldn't be bothered with it anymore. I was exhausted with imaging people and analyzing how they felt.

I titled my body over the ledge, ready to dive in. My back was hunched over as I looked below at the water. It was a dirty, murky looking river as they all were in New York. I wonder how hard it would be to retrieve my body? Would they even bother? I had to make it quick so there would be no hesitation. Paul was fast approaching and was now only a few yards away.

Do it! Molly whispered. *You'll never have to feel a thing again!*

Molly was somewhere behind me. I quickly glanced back and caught a glimpse of her nestled between two stopped cars whose occupants stared out at me in shock and horror. She had the usual hideously cruel grin on her face.

Oh Molly, if there was one thing, I was glad I no longer had to see, it was you. From the very first time I saw you I wished I never met you. You always encouraged me to kill myself. Even when it was my birthday. In the end, I guess we would both get what we wanted.

"Jayd, stop, please!" Paul called out. He was so close now.

Below me the water stirred and the sound caught my attention. Turning back around, I looked down only to see a figure emerge from the water and look right up at me. Their hair spilled out from around their face, floating on the surface of the water. The only thing I could see was their head and a pair of eyes. They glared up at me with cold, dead eyes. It was Melanie. Similar to the way I saw her sink downward when she had accepted her fate the day she drowned. Don't worry Melanie. I will soon be joining you. You won. You got your revenge.

Air filled my lungs as I took a deep breath and prepared to jump. I thought of Mama and Norman sitting at the kitchen table, waiting for me. It was the final comforting image I wanted in my mind. Paul was a few feet away from me now and I could feel his arms outstretched, waiting to grab me. And with one final exhale I jumped, hurling myself feet first into the water below. In that split second, I heard a mass of screaming and shock as people got out of their cars in panic.

"Oh my God!" someone shouted.

"Did you just see that?!" another shouted.

"Call the police! A girl just jumped!" came another voice.

"Jayd, Jesus Christ!" Paul yelled. "Grab my hand. Please!"

It took me a while to ask myself why I was still hearing these voices. To understand why I wasn't in the water and drowning. Why wasn't I submerged in dirty, icy water? Why hadn't Melanie grabbed a hold of me yet, pulling me down into the dark depths of silence and death? I glanced up in confusion, only to see my sweater yanked upward behind me and my entire stomach and back exposed. A large hole in my sweater was torn on a sharp edge that emerged from the lower ledge. It had been caught and ripped when I jumped from behind.

How fucking embarrassing. I couldn't even die right! And for the second time!

"Someone grab my legs! I can't reach her?" Paul called out. Why was he still trying? Oh Paul, you're such a good man. But it was pointless to waste your energy. His face looked into mine and his expression surprised me. Absolute concern, fear, and disbelief. He wasn't angry or smug. Paul really wanted to save me.

Someone on the bridge had grabbed a hold of his legs and he was lowered down–but still a few inches from my sweater despite stretching his body to full capacity.
I felt Melanie's anger from below.

"Jayd!" She yelled up. "Don't go with him! Come down here with me!" I looked away, back up into Paul's face.

Did he see her? Did he see his dead love?

Paul made no indication that he saw Melanie below as he continued to yell out to me and trying to grab ahold of my hand. I looked back down to see if Melanie was still there and she was now moving in a circular motion as she kept her eyes on me. My sweater was now slowly ripping from the pull of my weight. Soon it would rip entirely and I would go plugging below.

"Don't you see her, Paul?" I cried out to him. "Don't you see Melanie? She's right there! She wants me to die like she did Paul! Can't you see?

"Jayd! You have to grab my hand. You're too low for me to reach you!"

"Paul?" I yelled. "Can't you see Melanie?"

Paul paused and looked at me in fear and confusion. "Jayd, what are you talking about? Melanie's not here!"

Don't listen to him, Jayd! Melanie's below and she's waiting

"Jayd, please!" Paul shouted, trying to reach for my hand. I could hear the sirens up on the bridge. The police were here. Dozens of faces were emerging and looking down at me. I heard panic and crying. They all looked...worried. Were they all worried about me?

No, they're not, Jayd! They're disgusted in you! They want you to die! Now fall down!

Molly's face was among the crowd looking over the bridge. Unlike the others, she did not look worried. Molly was annoyed, agitated, and in her eyes…a look of desperation. I watched as she turned and disappeared from the crowd. The pull of my sweater was very uncomfortable. I reached up and grabbed the lower ledge, pulling myself upwards to offer some relief. My hand was only an inch from Paul's. I could easily reach him.

In that instance, Molly re-emerged and was now crouching down on the lower ledge, right above me. She grabbed my fingers and began pinching and pulling them off of the rail.

Let go! A monstrous roar came out of molly. My heart sped up and my body stiffened. Looking at Molly, I was terrified. It didn't even look like her anymore. Her skin looked gray and wrinkly and her eyes looked red. She looked like she was sick. Like she was dying.

"Jayydd!" Melanie called from the water below, "Do the right thing, Jayd!"

A life for a life! Molly whispered, as she continued to pry my fingers off from the rail. *Let go, Jayd! Please! I need you to let go!*

The emotions were overwhelming me now with everyone coming at me all at once. It was too much.

"Jayd, please!" Paul said. "I know how you feel, but understand that Melanie wouldn't want this!"

"How do you know?" I shot back up at him. "Paul, I killed your finance. It was my fault! How could I ever redeem myself?!"

"Jayd, please!" Paul pleaded. "You and I had no idea that it would happen that way. We're all victims. Melanie's death was an accident and it was tragic, but you shouldn't feel like it was your fault! I struggled with the guilt every day, but I know that it wasn't my fault either. Nor was it Melanie's. She was only doing what she felt was right. Only trying to help another, like she always did."

He's lying! Molly and Melanie roared in unison.

"Jayd, look at me!" Paul yelled. "Your life is just as precious as anyone else's. Just because you struggle to see that doesn't make it untrue. You are unique, and there's nothing wrong with that. That's the beauty of the world. We're all different and have our own paths in life. You have yet to discover yours!"

The police had now gathered on the bridge and a fire truck had emerged. The noise was deafening and I struggled to hear Paul as the scene became more chaotic by the second. They shouted orders to the crowd, many of whom were now outside of their cars. Traffic had come to a complete halt.

Molly made some kind of gurgling sound, as if she had been wounded and was struggling to stay awake and upright. What was happening?

"Come with me to Switzerland!" Paul yelled. "Jayd, please! I want you to come to Switzerland with me."
What? I said to myself. Why? Why would Paul want to go to Switzerland with me? I never even left New York. Not once in my life.

And if I went with Paul, would I regret this day for the rest of my life? If

I went with Paul, I would have to feel all the time. I would have to reflect the auras of the many faces I passed by in the streets. I would have to feel their emotions and be consumed by them, neglecting my own. I've been without my own emotions for so long, I no longer know what I truly feel or how to express myself. I would feel the tension in the room and the anger, and the sadness, and the happiness all at once. And then the overanalyzing and imaging would come in to make sense of it all. But my feet weren't truly on the ground and I wouldn't even know if I was right. Conversations would continue to be awkward and I would always be the target of animosity

I scared people. I made them uncomfortable. I couldn't connect with them and could barely communicate with them. I could figure them out, but they could never do the same for me. I understood and empathized with them against my will, and like a mirror image, reflected back what they were and what they felt. It was agonizing and it made me hate them just as much as they hated me.

I don't know myself and it scared me to the core. Would I like the real Jayd if I met her, and would she be accepted? Or would it be more of the same? I just didn't know what to expect. I wanted to be as sure as I was right now that death awaited me. I didn't want to live on the edge of life looking in as it passed me by while the world piled their emotions on me. I didn't want to drift in and out of reality and my subconscious mind– where sleep was my only reprieve. I didn't want to continue to hurt Mama or have to listen to Aunt Opal. I didn't want to drink my life away at Pat's or make no progress with Janelle. I didn't want to continue to have no friends or no social life at all. I don't want to continue being weird and lonely, Jayd.

I didn't want to think about Melanie every day and try to pitifully live for her and fail, as again, I was taking on another's persona instead of my own. I was trying to find closure where there wasn't any. Melanie was dead, and she wasn't coming back, no matter how much Paul and I wanted things to go differently on that day.

And despite all of this, despite not wanting to live the life of Jayd Broussard and my undying fear of the uncertainty of the future, I reached up and took Paul's hand.

NO! NO! NO! Molly roared, flailing her arms and tearing at her clothes. It was one of the most disturbing things I ever saw.

Oh c'mon, I thought. I'm not *that* bad to have around.

Chapter 30

"I think I honestly just wanted to stop feeling it all." I said, shoving another chocolate cookie into my mouth as I talked with my mouth full. "Everything hurt me, it would seem, more so than others. Not only was I always hypersensitive to what people said, their auras and any energy they emitted would engulf me. It was always like that, even when I was little. That "imaging" you said I did...I guess it was my way of explaining away what I felt by coming up with explanations. I can't really tell you why I did it Mama, but that's the best answer I can give you."

One after the other, I swallowed the large canister of mixed cookies Mama brought to the hospital as a treat for me. It was the day before I was to be discharged, and Mama and Aunt Opal had come to gather my things and get me ready to come home. With her beautiful brown almond eyes swallowing me with love, she sat beside me on my bed. Aunt Opal sat in a chair at the foot of the bed. She hardly looked at me or said anything, but as Mama and I chatted, I caught her glancing over at me a few times. With an expression of relief, guilt, and...warmth.

"Baby, I may never understand you," Mama said, now gripping me in a hug. I was smushed up against her neck and chest. She smelled so good, like flowers and spices. "But I want you to start talking to me, Jayd! From now on, you're going to tell me how you feel and what's going on inside your head every day! What you attempted to do! I almost had a heart attack!"

An overwhelming sense of guilt washed over me for putting Mama through that, but at the time, it seemed like the right decision to make. The only decision.

"I want you to try, Jayd. No more secrecy! Do you understand? Mama gripped me tighter. So tight that I could barely move. Her voice was stern, yet still full of love.

"Yes Mama, I understand." I told her, hugging her back.

Yes Mama, I understand. Molly said in an exaggerated mocking tone.

She was somewhere in my room, as she had been ever since I was admitted to the hospital, but I didn't care. I had enough of her. I was sick of the angry, desperate whispers begging me to kill myself and to go back to the bridge and jump or even throw myself out of my hospital room window beside my bed. She pleaded with me to harm myself and reiterated to me that no one loved me and that I was alone in the world.

"I have to go to the restroom and then make a few calls." Aunt Opal said, clearing her throat and getting up. "I'll be back." I watched her get up and take her bag, leaving behind her jacket. As she stood up, I had to again, as I usually did, marvel at how tall and shapely she was. She had such a beautiful body.

Aunt Opal nodded towards me and gave me a sad, tight-lipped smile and then a quick nod before turning around and heading out of the room. She closed the door swiftly behind her.
A deep sigh erupted from my chest and I looked at the floor. There was a moment of silence between me and Mama before she spoke.

"Y'know Jayd, Opal brought you those flowers." Mama said, gesturing towards the flowers brought in a few days ago that sat on the table beside my bed. "And when she heard what had happened, she raced back home in a panic. Jayd, when I tell you she was hysterical. The police had to be called to calm her down." Mama looked me in the eyes as she said this. "She thought you had died. We both did. And although I was completely out of my mind, I have to say that I never saw Opal that way for as long as we were sisters."

Aunt Opal? Crying? Hysterical? About me? I couldn't believe it. What reality had I woken up to?
As if she felt my skepticism, Mama continued.

"It's true Jayd, and it even shocked me." Mama was now sitting up against the headboard and I leaned on her shoulder. "And look baby, I know how you feel about Aunt Opal, and you have every right too. But I want you to know that Aunt Opal does love and care about you. She's just very jaded about life and can be a bully sometimes. But she loves you and she told me so. She just…can't understand you. And it frustrates her."

Get in line, I thought to myself.

I had long decided Aunt Opal was my enemy, but as Mama spoke, I tried to give Aunt Opal the benefit of the doubt. And have some empathy for her. It was, after all, what I was known to do. Maybe one day in the future we could see eye to eye.

The fresh, shaven head of a handsome man poked through the door. His honey-colored eyes scanned the room quickly before they fell on mine. In his hand was a bouquet of flowers. Upon seeing him, Mama jumped up from the bed, her cheeks red from blush with a look of pleasant surprise.

"Mr. McPhearson! Hello!" Mama exclaimed. "Are you here to see Jayd?"

Paul cleared his throat and gave Mama a smile.

"Sorry to interrupt…I tried to visit Jayd earlier, but they wouldn't let me see her until now." Our eyes met, and for a moment, I felt butterflies in my stomach. I looked down at my bed covers.

"Oh, it's not a problem!" Mama told Paul. "Her Aunt and I weren't permitted for some time and then afterwards only close family were allowed. Why don't you come in and I'll give you two some time to talk! Oh, and are those for Jayd?"

Mama gestured to the flowers that Paul was holding and reached for them. Paul handed her the flowers, which were a bunch of gorgeous white roses, and shoved them into the vase with the flowers Aunt Opal brought earlier. She turned around quickly facing me, gave me a peck on the head and headed out.

"I'll go find your aunt and we'll go pick you up some food!" Mama called back as she exited the room and shut the door.

The room was still and quiet. Paul walked over and sat in Aunt Opal's chair. He took off his jacket and put it behind the chair. He wore a sweater vest, some dress pants and shoes. I caught a glimpse of something shimmering on his earlobe. I spoke first.

"You got a piercing?" I asked him in surprise and pointed to the small diamond earring I saw wedged in his left ear. Paul was caught off guard, and then chuckled.

"Yeah!" he said, a little embarrassed. His cheeks turned bright pink. "I thought I would try something new. Something different."

I watched him for a moment and then gave a smile. "I like it." I told him. "It looks good on you"

"Thanks Jayd," Paul replied, rubbing his piercing. "Still hurts like hell, though"

Silence drifted between. He spoke next.

"How have you been Jayd?" he asked, hesitantly and gently. Paul tilted forward and rested his arm at the end of my bed. "Are you still…" He drifted off, not wanting to say the word out loud. So, I decided to help him out.

"Still suicidal?" I said, finishing his sentence.

"Paul looked down, and nodded his head.

"I guess…no. Not really." I told him. "I'm kind of coming to terms with it all, Paul. Slowly, but surely."

"I think something still wants me to be here," I told him. "Maybe that something is me or maybe it's fate. Maybe…I never wanted to die at all. I don't know what the answer is, but I don't think it's death."

Suddenly, to the right side of my view I caught a glimpse of a ghastly figure appearing. If I hadn't instantly recognized who it was, I would have screamed out in horror. Molly, or what used to be Molly, stood beside my bed, fists clenched, and red eyes wildly bulging out of her head. Her skin was drooping and gray and her hair was wild. Her once pretty dress was sloppily ripped, as if she had torn it to shreds with her bare hands. Scars lined her arms and legs and face. And her entire body had become more and more translucent since the day I pulled myself up from the ledge.

She looked horrible, like an undead monster. Day by day as she appeared to taunt me, she would descend into this horrid creature that stood before me, but this time…this time she was barely recognizable. It was as if Molly was morphing into something out of my worst nightmare–or hers.

Desperation and sheer panic clouded her expression. Grabbing the covers of my bed sheet, she pulled at me weakly. She slammed her hands on my side table, then once on the headboard of my bed, and then on the top of her own head repeatedly. She looked like she was suffocating. Like a helpless, pitiful, dying, animal. All I could do was watch. I knew, and Molly knew.

This was the end of the road for her.

She didn't succeed at whatever her purpose was, and now she was withering away. Molly, the menace of my mind, was dying.

"Jayd…it wasn't your fault," Paul said gently. His tone sounded as if he were pleading for me to believe it. "Melanie would have done the same for anyone. She was selfless and kind hearted. We weren't right for each other, but she was a wonderful person. She did what she thought was the right thing and you shouldn't hold any guilt for that. She would've been proud of herself, and you for not letting go off that ledge."

I listened to him and let his words simmer, digesting his intent.

"I'm not sure about that, Paul." I finally told, and it was the best truth that I could give him. "I don't know if it wasn't truly my fault."

To the side of me Molly began screaming erratically in my face. In Paul's face. Only nothing came out. It was as if she had been muted. She ran to the walls of the room and banged on them. She banged on the windows, and on the door, and on the floor. Yet, I heard nothing. As I watched her mentally explode and break down, I felt my chest getting lighter and my mind become clearer.

"Jayd, I know that you have guilt, and, unfortunately, may carry it forever, but I want you to know that you're not alone in it." Paul's hand rested on my knee, just below the hospital gown I wore. "There are so many things I wish I could take back about that day, but I know that I can't and that's why I try to focus on the things I can do. I try to live my life to the fullest as best I can. Before, I tried to live like Melanie and do the things that she would get me to do and the things that she was passionate about. I thought to myself…if I try to live for Melanie, maybe a part of me can be redeemed. If I could just do the things she did, and go to the places we went together, she could still be here with me…somehow. Maybe I could connect with her again. Maybe I could get back the joy I had when we were together, like in old photos of us. Maybe I could get…closure."

Tears ran down his cheeks as he talked, and the painful irony of it all wasn't lost on me. This entire time, we were both consumed with guilt and trying to live for the dead woman we both felt responsible for.

"But that closure just wouldn't come. No matter what I did I always felt that I was stealing the life that she should be living…and felt that I was neglecting living my own."

Was that why I didn't succeed? I thought to myself as Paul talked. Was it because I was trying to be what Melanie was which went beyond merely doing the things that she did? Why did I think that I could become an entire other human being? Was it because I failed to realize that Melanie was Melanie and Jayd was Jayd? That I was further subjecting myself to her existence as a form of self-inflicted trauma? I did want to forget what had happened, because that means that I would eventually forget about Melanie. And I didn't think that I deserved that privilege.

So, was I just punishing myself all along, with no closure in sight? And what was closure anyway? Was it getting over that day and moving on or was it simply acting as if it never happened? Was it coming to terms that it did in fact happen and that I couldn't change things, or was it reminding myself each and every day that I should be thankful that I was still here? Was Paul and Melanie's forgiveness the closure I needed? Did I need Melanie to rise from the grave and tell me that everything was going to be okay, and that she forgives me?

I don't know. Maybe it was all or none of these things.

I handed Paul a tissue and he wiped away his tears. He cleared his throat and sniffled. His crying was both endearing and made me feel awkward. I knew how he felt, but wasn't sure how to truly comfort him. We both seemed to have that problem.

"I'm glad I met you, Jayd" he said, looking into my eyes.

Molly rolled her now completely see-through form over the bed, between Paul and I. She stood up and hopped up and down on the bed, pathetically trying to get my attention. She knelt down and grabbed my shoulders, and shook them. I felt a faint pressure where her hands were. Looking me dead in the eyes, Molly desperately pleaded with me. She pleaded with me to look at her, to notice and pay attention to her, to recognize and feel for her. To save her. And I could honestly say that in that very moment, I had never felt so emotionless. So indifferent.

So unempathetic.

With a final glare, I looked into my long-time tormentor's eyes as she, or rather it, pleaded with me one final time before she completely vaporized in front of me. I neither jumped nor flinched.

There was nothing left, not even a scent or feeling. I looked at the space where Molly had been only a moment ago. Not a single particle could be seen. She had completely evaporated out of existence.

It was so sudden and instant, as if Molly was never here. Not in my mind or in reality. Tears streamed down my face as I inhaled. A relief like no other came over me and the heaviness that long plagued me... was gone. The never-ending feeling of fear and misery had vanished without a trace. I didn't feel closed in or off anymore. Inside, something had awakened.

Paul hadn't taken his eyes off me, and now looked at me with a look of confusion and concern.

"I think it's time that we move on Paul." I told him, smiling through my tears. I turned back to look at him. I looked into a handsome face that was full of worry and sadness. I didn't like Paul worrying about me, so I thought to put a smile on his face.

"I think it's finally time we put all this to rest, Paul," I told him, "Together". He matched my smile with his as he reached forward and we embraced.

Chapter 31

"So, your mother tells me that you're starting school in two weeks. Is that true?" Janelle asked over the phone and between sips of her beverage.

"Yes!" I replied, happy she asked. It was about time we talked about something else besides my second attempt at taking my life. "It's at the local community college. I'm starting a little late, but I have my classes picked out and the syllabus of each class was sent yesterday. I'll be ok."

"That's great Jayd! I'm glad you're getting back on track. School and perhaps becoming more involved and social will be good for you."

My classes consisted of English, art, sociology, anthropology and psychology classes. Mama and I picked them out together. Writing more and expressing myself either through creative writing and art was what we both thought would be therapeutic and fun. I still had no idea what I wanted to be, what career goals I wanted to accomplish, or even where I saw myself in the next five years.

"Take it day by day, Jayd" Janelle had said. "You can figure that out as you go."

I chose psychology, sociology, and anthropology, because I wanted... or rather I needed to get a better understanding on who I was if I was going to accept and continue to live my life as I have been. What really is imaging and how does it develop? Can one be too empathetic or is the world just lacking in empathy? What made me so introverted, observant, and afraid? Was it childhood trauma or something genetic? There were so many questions that I long pondered and would now be seeking the answers to.

"That sounds awesome, Jayd!" Paul had said when I told him about the classes I was going to take. "You'll be like Chiron, the wounded healer."

"Chiron?" I asked in confusion. "What's that?"

"It's just a character based on a Greek myth. In the myth, Chiron is wounded but learns to heal himself, and in turn, learns to heal others. He becomes a wounded healer."

"Oh, I see..." I replied. "I didn't think of it that way? Who could I help?"

"Jayd, you could help many people." Paul had said. "As you learn about yourself, I'm sure you'll find others who share your same experiences. Even at your group sessions, I see a lot of similarities between you and others."

I nodded at him in agreement, but in my head, I thought to myself that there was no way I could heal others. I wasn't even sure I was healed or would ever be completely healed myself. The future was truly a mystery, and most times I thought it was best to not even think of it. To just live in the present, in the moment, and for once, out of my head.

I sat back against my headboard and reached down and stroked Norman's head. He was curled up in a ball and fast asleep. Soft purrs floated up to me. Still in my pajamas, I gently got up and went to my window. Peeking outside I could see the leaves now completely losing their green color. Mellow winds pushed the leaves from their branches and they rolled down the streets and on top of cars and houses. There were a few people out and about and the birds were noisily chirping as well as the squirrels running in circles on the ground.

I closed my window and pulled the blinds. Putting my feet inside my slippers, I headed for the door and exited my room, tip-toeing so as not to make too much noise. Our apartment was so tiny and the doors so old, they creaked and the sounds could even be heard from the hallways. I went into the kitchen and sat down at the table. Mama had her back to me and was effortlessly gliding from stove to sink and back. She wore a purple, silk nightgown and had her hair up.

The kitchen smelled of bacon, potatoes, and cinnamon. She was making my favorite breakfast dish; french toast, bacon, and home fries.

"Good morning, Mom!" I said and gave her a quick peck on the cheek. She whirled around and looked at me in surprise.

"Mom?", she comically crossed her arms and huffed. "Since when did you start calling me Mom? She asked. "What happened to Mama?"

"Oh, I don't know." I told her. "I figured that it sounds a little too kiddish"

Mama gave an exaggerated offended look and I chuckled. She turned back to cooking and I sat down at the table.

"You want one or two french toasts?" she asked, humming to the beat of a song that played on the radio and was far before my time.

"Three!" I replied. Mama rolled her eyes and a chuckle escaped from her lips.

Beside the sink and under the shelves was a coffee pot smoking. I sat back in my chair and savored the delicious scents.
"Yea...," I continued on the phone with Janelle. "I may try to join a few clubs. Meet new people. There's bound to be a few weird kids out there like

me. I snickered, letting Janelle know that I wasn't serious with that remark.

"I'm also going to start going back to those sessions with Paul. He invited me to go this afternoon, so we'll be meeting up later."

"Wonderful!" Janelle exclaimed. "I'm so proud of you Jayd! You're like a different person from the one I first met. I can barely recognize your voice, it's full of life and excitement."

A small smile crossed my lips even though I knew Janelle couldn't see it. I did feel a little different.

Ok, I'm lying.

I felt a LOT different. And it felt amazing. And strange, and a little scary. But in a good way. I felt…no I knew…that everything was going to be okay.

"Are you still working?" Janelle suddenly asked. "I know you were concerned about medical bills and money was tight for your family."

"I am," I replied. "I'm still working at Sylvia's, although I'm looking for another part time job.

"Wow," Janelle responded. "That's good. But, well, don't overdo it Jayd. You're young and have plenty of time and life left in you. Take it easy and don't forget to practice self-care and take care of your mental health. That's the most important thing. It was great talking to you and I'll see you next week!"

We said our goodbyes and I hung up just as Aunt Opal came into the kitchen. For a second, our eyes met, and then we looked away. It had been like that ever since I got home. It was progress, I guess. At least we weren't arguing anymore.

"Good morning, Aunt Opal!" I said, giving her a smile.

She sat down, opposite me. By the counter, Mama took out a mug and began pouring coffee.
"Good morning, Jayd!" she said, as Mama placed a cup of coffee in front of her. "And thank you Ruby!". I watched as she scrolled through her phone, looking at the news as she always did.

Mama went back to the counter and continued to cook and hum. I hummed along with her, nodding side to side.

"Got any plans today, Jayd?" Aunt Opal asked, not looking up from her phone.

"Yes!" I said. "I'm meeting up with Paul later and we'll go out to lunch afterwards. It'll be my treat. Because, y'know, it's the least I can do knowing he covered all of my medical bills.

"Oh, that's right!" Mama exclaimed near the stove. "Jayd, you must invite Paul over to dinner and we'll all chip in for a gift for him. That was an amazing thing he did for us!"

"Uh no. He said it's alright." I told her. "No gifts, I'll just treat him out today when we meet up. That's all."

But Mama held her hand up in defiance and I knew what that meant.

So, dinner and a gift it was. No discussion. I turned back to Aunt Opal.

"I'm going to start doing those group sessions again with Paul regularly. We have a meeting later today."

"Hmm," Aunt Opal mused. "That sounds nice. Well, enjoy yourself!"

I again sat back in my chair and browsed online with my phone. Grumbles erupted from my stomach and the smells in the kitchen were driving me crazy. My mouth was watery and my throat dry.

"Mom!" I asked her. "How long until breakfast is done? I'm starving!"

"Give me a few minutes, Jayd!" she said, turning her head and looking back at me.

Aunt Opal caught her eyes and in the corner of vision, I could see them looking at each other.

"Mom??" Aunt Opal mouthed in confusion.

"I know?!" Mama mouthed back.

Chapter 32

I stood in front of the large, marble headstone, marveling at it. It was wide, and looked like it weighed a ton. Engraved on the front were delicate flowers, similar to the many laid on the ground in front of the grave. I reached out my arm and ran my fingers along the top edge. It felt perfectly sculpted, with not a rough edge in sight. I then moved my hand along the front of the headstone. It was smooth; and I thought to myself how expensive it must have been and how she deserved nothing less. I sighed, as my eyes drifted below to the writing that had been carved. *Here Lies the Lovely and Magnificent Melanie Medela. Beloved Daughter. Forever and always in the hearts and memories of many.* Her birthdate and death were carved last.

At that very moment, a small robin landed on the edge of Melanie's grave. Facing me, it bent its legs and chirped. I watched as it turned side to side and back and forth as it continued to chirp. It looked at me, and for a moment, we stared at one another. It then began hopping back and forth, until it opened its wings and flew away, gone just as fast as it had arrived.

Was that you Melanie? I thought to myself.

A breeze swam through the air and I shivered, pulling my jacket tighter around me and lowering my hoodie. Paul was still back in the car waiting for me. I told him that I would like some time alone at Melanie's gravesite and he obliged. Holding the bouquet of petunias in one hand, I carefully knelt down and placed the flowers next to the many that sat neatly on the ground. Paul let me know that petunias were one of Melanie's favorite flowers. I had brought a mixture of red, white, and purple.

Despite being gone, Melanie's gravesite had to be the liveliest and most eye-catching in the entire cemetery. She was so loved and still fabulous in death as she was in life.

What I had come here to say, I wasn't completely sure. I had gone over in my head and written down so many words that I could say to Melanie, but none of it seemed to authenticate what I truly needed and wanted to convey. I decided to just say whatever came to mind.

"Melanie, first and foremost, I want to thank you. Not only did you save my life that day, but you helped me develop into a different person. You helped me see that maybe there are things in life worth living for. That there were places out there worth seeing and people out there worth meeting."

"I wish that we could have met in different circumstances, perhaps we would have become friends. For the past months, I have suffered with immense guilt over your death, and I still have not fully healed from it. Perhaps I never will. Perhaps when I think of you a pang of guilt and sadness will follow. But that's ok. I'm only human, and if you were to get to know me you would see that I tend to wear my heart on my sleeve. Always have and always will."

"Paul says that I shouldn't feel guilty. That it wasn't my fault and that I am just as much of a victim as you are. Deep down I know that he's right, but I cannot help but think if I hadn't been there that day and if you hadn't seen me, you would still be alive. Paul also carries guilt about that day and what happened between you two. In the end, all I can say is that, more than anything, I wish I could turn back time and stop what happened. But I know I can't, and there's no use torturing myself with that revelation. For so long, I felt that you should be here, and not me. You were optimistic and loved and had and would have accomplished so much more in life. I thought there was no way that I could compare, and that it was I, and I alone, who should have died that day."

"Regarding me, I don't believe that much anymore. There is a place for me, somewhere out there, maybe even here, that I haven't discovered yet. I have a purpose, even if I don't see it now. Melanie, I'm sorry about what happened to you, and I thank you every day for the sacrifice that you made. Please know that you'll never be forgotten and that you will always be missed by those who knew you. You left a tremendous mark on many people's lives, especially mine. Paul loves and misses you, and I miss you even though I didn't know you. Rest in eternal peace."

With that, I dried away my tears and turned around, heading back to the car where Paul was waiting. When I got in, he asked if I was okay, noticing my stained sweater and wet cheeks. I told him I was fine, and that I think I finally found a bit of closure that I needed.

When we drove away, I spotted, or at least I think I spotted the little robin again. It was perched on the gate, chirping at us as we drove by. I turned to smile gently at it before it disappeared from view.

Chapter 33

The chatter and noise of the airport muffled the words that Paul was yelling out to me. I stretched over from my chair and leaned into him.

"What was that?" I asked him.

He smiled, and motioned towards his bag.

"I got something for you!" he exclaimed.

"Oh no, Paul!" I told him, slightly embarrassed. "I told you, you don't have to buy me anything. This trip is honestly enough. I've never been outside of New York!"

Paul waved his hand as if to say nonsense, and began digging into his bag. I sat in my chair, tapping my heels against the floor. Across from us sat a family of four. The mother and little girl that she had on her lap smiled over at me and I smiled back.

"I like your outfit!" the mom said to me. I blushed.

"Thank you!" I replied. So apparently Mama and Aunt Opal were right. They had fussed all morning at me, trying to get me to wear a skirt and heels instead of my usual tee-shirt, jeans, and sneakers combo. I gave in and wore the outfit they picked out. I surprised myself, Paul included, with how nice I looked. The mom was the third stranger to compliment me.

"So…Switzerland…" I said, leaning over back into Paul. "I wonder how it'll be?"

"No clue!" he replied, still searching his bag. "I heard they have gorgeous scenery and nice historic towns. The closest I've ever been was Germany."

I had butterflies in my stomach, and it wasn't from anything Paul said or did, or from my nervousness about the trip. All of the feelings were coming back; mine's, Paul's, and everyone else at this enormous airport. I felt overjoyed, nauseous, impatient, excited, upset, and anxious, all at once. It was, as it always was, overwhelming. Before I freaked out I paused and inhaled. Janelle had told me what I could try to do whenever this happened.

"Take a deep breath, Jayd. Take a deep breath and drown out all the noise, close your eyes and find yourself. Ask yourself what you truly feel at the moment and recognize that everything that you're feeling is not your own. Once you do that, you'll learn to adjust and even block out certain emotions that don't serve you. Even more, you'll get to the root cause of why you're feeling certain emotions."

As I remembered what she said, I calmed down and thought about how excited and curious I should be about his upcoming trip, along with an amazing person I was going on this trip with. This would be an adventure, and not a burden.

And it was time that I started seeing life that way

"Can all first class passengers boarding flight 69 come to the gate!" called the female announcer. Paul and I jumped up simultaneously.

"Oh, that's us! Let's go!" I said, pulled at him.

"Hang on, hang on!" Paul chuckled. "I want to give this to you before we board." Out of his knapsack, he pulled out a small white box and handed it to me. I hesitantly took the box and looked up at him.

"Paul...I said you don't have to get me anything! This is too much! I bemoaned.

"Just open it!" he said, gesturing towards the box.

I unwrapped the bow and opened the box. Sitting inside, right in the middle, was the same jade that Paul had shown me earlier, only this time, it was linked around a diamond and silver chain. I gasped. It was the most beautiful necklace I had ever laid eyes on.

Before Paul could explain, I jumped into his arms and embraced him into a bear hug. A flurry of people bumped into me from behind.

"Alright, thank you Paul, but that's it!" I laughed. We headed for the gate before I stopped in my tracks. Paul paused as well and looked back at me.

"Hey, what's wrong? He asked, concerned.

Standing still I tuned the world out and waited. My eyes shifted from corner to corner, from ceiling to floor, behind and in front of me. I searched and waited for her to appear. I waited for her heartless laugh to erupt in my mind, her obnoxious twirling, and her cruel words. I waited for the face that looked identical to mine to appear and torment me. To appear as she had done so many times before and taunt me and tell me that she was never going away. That I was a fool to think that I had rid myself of her. That we were one, and she would always be with me until the day I died. I stood silently and waited, where every second seemed like an hour.

But nothing happened, and she never appeared.

Like the static of white noise, a void of emptiness and nothingness filled the space where she once existed in the depths of my mind. I breathed a sigh of relief, and turned back to Paul who was now looking at me with deep concern. I gave him a huge smile, linked my arm into his, and pulled him forwards, towards the rush of people.

"Paul, my dear, let's go!" I said to him, "It's a new world out there waiting for us!"